"You are hiding something... This is not in my head, Cassie," he said, standing up.

"What is that supposed to mean?"

"A normal person doesn't go to extreme lengths to make sure their restaurant isn't featured in the paper or reviewed," Ryan ranted. "A chef of your caliber should covet the attention that Mama Gina's is getting, but instead, you're threatening to close up shop. You claim to come from Ann Arbor, Michigan, yet you know nothing about its festivals, never biked or hiked any of its world-class trails." He turned, pointing at her bookshelves. "You have no family pictures, photo albums or even mementos from past trips. There is nothing in this house that goes beyond your years in Bakerton. If I didn't know better, I'd ask if you're in WITSEC."

"What?" The shock at hearing him say the words registered on her face, and she played it to her advantage. "You're being ridiculous. I'm just a private person."

"It's more than that. You're hiding from someone, and from the terror I saw on your face earlier, I think that someone has come to Bakerton."

Jacqueline Adam is a married author from British Columbia and a mom to two incredible children. She and her family love to find adventure, whether it be zip-lining, riding roller coasters or camping throughout the Rocky Mountains and beyond. Jackie writes Love Inspired Suspense stories with strong, dynamic characters that overcome impossible odds.

Books by Jacqueline Adam

Love Inspired Suspense

Targeted Witness

Targeted Witness

Jacqueline Adam

LOVE INSPIRED® SUSPENSE
INSPIRATIONAL ROMANCE

Recycling programs for this product may not exist in your area.

ISBN-13: 978-1-335-58815-9

Targeted Witness

For questions and comments about the quality of this book, please contact us at CustomerService@Harlequin.com.

Love Inspired
22 Adelaide St. West, 41st Floor
Toronto, Ontario M5H 4E3, Canada
www.LoveInspired.com

Printed in U.S.A.

Come unto me, all ye that labour and are heavy laden,
and I will give you rest.
—*Matthew* 11:28

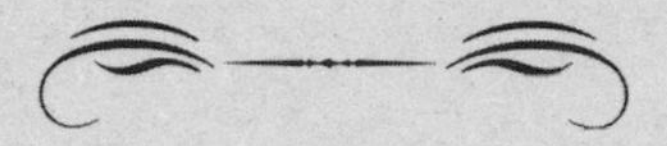

This book is dedicated to God, my family and friends.
Thank you for all the love, encouragement,
chocolate and support over the years.
This book would not have been possible without you.

ONE

Cassie Whitfield locked the main door to her Italian restaurant and paused, her key still in the lock. She wanted to blame the chill down her spine on the wind, but her WITSEC training balked at such easy soothing. With a sigh, she cast a furtive gaze up the historic Main Street, which had long since closed for the night, and tugged her white knit hat low over her ears. There were no strange movements from the shadows, no unusual sounds. Everything was just as it should be. Cassie pulled her coat tighter. Exhaustion was getting the better of her. After all, this was small-town Bakerton, and nothing ever happened here.

With a shake of her shoulders, Cassie dismissed the lingering unease and watched the lightly falling December snow as she walked up the street toward her Jeep. The delicate flakes had begun dusting the dark green business awnings and framing the old brick and stucco buildings in a festive white. Whenever it snowed in Bakerton, the town couldn't help but look like a porcelain Christmas village, especially once the white lights and green garlands were hung. It was one of the things Cassie loved about living here.

Exhausted after a long day of cooking, she climbed into her old Jeep and turned the key only to hear the engine emit a plaintive growl. "Come on," she murmured as her dash came alive with amber and red lights. She tried again, but her vehicle only sputtered more stubbornly.

Cassie slumped back in her seat. All she wanted to do was go home, soak in a nice, hot tub and crawl into bed. *Was that too much to ask?* Cassie dared a glance toward the Main Street clock.

The soft yellow glow cast from the streetlamps gave just enough light to read the time. While it wasn't midnight yet, it was close enough, and everyone she knew would be fast asleep this late on a Monday night. Cassie stared out her window as a thought began teasing the edges of her mind.

She could call Ryan. He'd probably be starting his patrol shift right about now.

The simple idea was all it took to imagine the scene. Her ex-boyfriend would pull up in his police cruiser. His tall, muscular frame would get out of the car, and he'd stand adjusting his hat, trying to tame the tendrils of scruffy blond hair from sneaking beneath its edges. Then he would level those direct blue eyes on her. Eyes that held so many questions about her past and thinly veiled the hostility he felt toward her evasive answers.

Despite Ryan's feelings, he would help her because that was the type of guy he was—kind, loyal and dedicated. She sighed. While those traits, coupled with his rugged good looks, made him irresistible, they also produced a cop with an uncanny sense when something was off, and because of that, her cover story was something he could never stop doubting. It was like a mosquito bite that he just had to itch. All conversations led to questions about her past, and her vague answers only created more tension between them.

No, she thought, resolved. She didn't need Ryan's help. She could manage well enough on her own.

While Cassie didn't love the idea of walking home, especially on a cold night like tonight, there wasn't much of a choice. She burrowed her hands into her pockets and headed down Main Street at a brisk pace.

When she reached Polson Park, Cassie went

down to the paved trail that tracked alongside the Powder River. The path was one of her favorites this time of year, with its snow-laced maple trees and wrought iron lampposts decorated with bright red bows. Maybe walking home wasn't so bad, after all.

With a continued hustle in her step, Cassie had rounded the first bend into the woods when her feet slipped sideways, sending her purse flying. Unable to save herself, she landed with a hard thud on her hip and twisted her knee. Instant agony shot down her leg while icy snow cascaded over the collar of her coat and slid down her shirt, nipping at her skin. Winded, she lay still, bearing the stinging cold until she regained her breath.

A soft crunch of footsteps broke into the quiet night.

Surprised, Cassie sat up, jarring her knee. Curious who would emerge from the darkness, Cassie twisted to look behind her, but the footsteps stopped.

"Hello?" she called out into the gloom and waited for a response. When no one answered, she called out again. "If someone's there, I could really use some help," she said, her pulse quickening. "Hello?"

A tree branch, somewhere outside the reach of the path light, gave a soft snap, sending a warning chill through her. Her senses honed, she sat listening, but no other sounds came except for the burble from the river.

She shook her head and dusted off her mitts. *Don't be a ninny. It's probably just a deer.*

Cassie hoisted herself onto her feet. Pain seared like a hot fire through her knee, pulling a hiss from her lips. She managed to limp to a nearby bench and then eased herself down.

It's not going to be that easy today, is it, God? Cassie scanned the path for her purse, but there was no sign of it. If only she had called a friend when she had the opportunity. Tenderly, she bent her leg. Nothing was broken, but that didn't mean it was going to be a pleasant walk home either. She grimaced. One thing was for sure, sitting here wasn't getting her anywhere.

After traveling a short ways down the path, Cassie slowed her pace. A feeling of being watched prickled the back of her neck. Careful to appear casual, she surveilled the dark. Nothing moved among the evergreens and barren maples. Everything seemed as it should, yet something in the woods wasn't right.

A damp fog began rolling in around her, dimming the glow from the path lights. The woods were becoming thicker, but Cassie knew she didn't dare turn back. Not wanting to dawdle, she increased her pace when the sound of footsteps rose again. She paused, pulse racing, and looked over her shoulder. A large male figure emerged from the deep shadow with an oversize hood obscuring his face. From the way he was moving, she could tell this was no Good Samaritan.

Fear shot up Cassie's spine like fireworks, catapulting her down the trail. Agony tore through her knee, but she ignored it, instead pushing herself to go faster.

Her mind spiraled with terror as she ran. After all these years, had the assassin who had forced her into WITSEC finally found her? Her breathing turned ragged, but she refused to slow down, her thoughts focusing on escape.

Cassie knew she was coming up to the fork in the path. If she took the trail to the left, it would take her to the suspension bridge over the Powder River, with her house and safety on the other side. The path to the right would lead her to Hughes Lane, a place where people might or might not be around. Neither option was great. *God, please help me.*

A dog barked in the distance, and Cassie jumped. She dared to look over her shoulder and froze with a scream on her lips.

The man was closing the distance between them at an alarming rate. Running was futile, but she kept on. Would he kill her outright? Or would he force her onto the bridge and throw her over the side, making it look like an accident and preventing any further testimony? Her mind filled with images of falling, crashing through the thin ice and being submerged under the glacial river waters.

Cassie curled her hands into fists. Whcther this was a mugging or an assassination attempt, there was no way she was going down without a fight. She stopped her stumbling and turned to face him, her chest heaving.

"What do you want?" she yelled.

The male figure stopped, not even twenty feet behind her, and stood stock-still. Then, his hands moved casually into his pockets, and a low haunting whistle played from his lips.

Unnerved, Cassie launched off the pathway. She half ran, half limped through the trees. Barren shrubs clawed at her clothes, and crusty drifts of snow spilled into her boots, but she didn't notice. Pushing through the wintry brush, Cassie burst into the intersection of Hughes and Kirkway. She stood for a moment turning in all directions, looking for any sign of another human being, gasping for breath. Suddenly, she was bathed in flashing blue lights.

Relief flooded her. She bent over, trying to breathe, trying to get ahold of herself.

She was safe. Oh, thank God, she was safe. Tears welled in her eyes, and she swiped at them with her dirty white mitt, willing her heart to stop pounding. Without even looking, Cassie knew who would be in that cruiser and for once, she didn't care.

"Cassie?" Ryan Matherson rushed to her side, leaving his police cruiser door wide open.

She threw her arms around him and buried her face into his chest. The smell of him, a mix of polished wood and leather, overpowered her senses. Held in his strong arms, she felt safe. She didn't even consider pulling away. She just needed a moment—a moment to drink in his strength, a moment to pull herself together.

"What happened?" he said, softly tucking a long strand of her auburn hair behind her ear. "Are you okay?"

No. She wasn't okay. She was far from okay, but instead of falling apart like she wanted to, Cassie stepped back and trained her eyes on his car. Ryan might be her ex-boyfriend, but the magnetic pull she felt toward him would never change. Keeping an emotional distance between them was like putting up a wood fence and expecting it to keep out a forest fire.

Cassie took a calming breath and looked up

into Ryan's worried blue eyes, trying for a casual smile. No facade she could ever put up would withstand his scrutiny. However, there was no other option but to try.

"Yeah," Cassie said, giving a laugh that sounded fake even to her own ears. "Just a victim of an overactive imagination." His eyes narrowed, so she quickly switched topics. "I understand that this is awkward, but do you think you could give me a ride home? I twisted my knee back there, and it's killing me."

Ryan looked down at her torn dress pants. His eyes met hers, sending a ripple of warmth cascading through her. When his steady arm came around her shoulders, Cassie readily leaned into him, for once accepting the safe shelter he offered. Together, they moved toward his cruiser.

Unable to stop herself, Cassie glanced toward the dark forest behind them. Her body began to tremble. Without saying a word, Ryan tucked her closer to him.

"I can't remember the last time we've had a December that's been this cold," she said.

Ryan tilted his head, his words deliberately soft. "What happened in the woods?"

"I feel silly," she said, feigning embarrassment.

"Cassie?"

She stared up at the rigid set of his stubbled jaw. Her throat tightened while her mind raced to think of what she should say about what had just happened. WITSEC protocols were rigid, and as much as she wanted to, she couldn't break them. She couldn't tell Ryan about her past and the things she had witnessed eight years ago. But on the other hand, how could she send Ryan unprepared, chasing through the woods after a renowned assassin?

Her stomach felt heavy with what she had to do. Protocol required that the truth be abbreviated. Maybe she could make it sound innocent enough that he wouldn't go running after shadows. Cassie closed her eyes and remembered the coaching she'd received in her WITSEC training.

The words raced out of her mouth. "My Jeep wouldn't start, so I was walking home, and I thought I heard something." She let out an awkward sigh. "Anyways, I spooked and slipped and well, you saw the rest."

Ryan's eyes locked on her face, and she wished the ground would open up and swallow her whole. They stood at the cruiser, his jaw tightening. His gaze left hers and stared past her to the small wooded area where she had emerged moments before. When he drew his eyes back to her, his frigid stare left no doubt that he saw through the story.

"You should warm up inside the car. You're like ice." He abruptly took his arm from her shoulder and opened the passenger door, holding it wide. "Get in the car, Cassie," Ryan said, his deep voice tinged with forcefulness.

Words hung on her lips, but she bit them back. Already she could feel him putting up the emotional wall that divided them. His response shouldn't have surprised her, and yet it stung all the same. She turned her face from his and got into the car. His thumb pressed down on the lock with a thunk.

"Ryan—" her eyes darted to his "—don't. You're not going to find anything."

He didn't respond. He just shut the door, leaving Cassie speechless while he crossed the street and stepped into the bush, disappearing from sight.

What was he thinking going in there all alone? Her bluster immediately faded, the answer making her feel sick. He'd gone in there alone because she hadn't told him everything. He had no idea what could be lurking in those woods. Her eyes searched the forest where he had disappeared, looking for any faint hint of motion. Cassie glanced at the clock. Well, if he didn't return soon, she'd just have to go in after him. She let out a slow breath and began praying for his protection.

Thankfully, he emerged from the trees moments later and strode toward the cruiser. Keeping his head bent against the wind, Ryan carried something in his hands. A swirl of snow flew into the car when he sat in the driver's seat. Unceremoniously, he dropped her purse onto her lap.

"I'm driving you home," he said.

Cassie muttered a thank-you.

When they turned onto the highway, the click of the car signal only seemed to punctuate the growing rift between them. His silence thundered with questions about her past that had been asked many times before and clumsily deflected. Cassie knew it wouldn't matter what she said. His cop mind was never going to stop pursuing truthful answers or wondering why she was withholding information.

She cleared her throat, despising the crackling tension in the air. If her best friend and coworker, Sarah Connelly, could see her now, she'd be telling Cassie to at least talk to the man. Her fingers toyed with her purse. "You're still welcome to come into the restaurant. Sarah misses seeing you."

At first, Cassie thought he meant to ignore her, but then he whispered, "Just Sarah?"

Her breath caught. She didn't want to answer, but it was the one question she could be truthful with. Her cheeks grew warm, and she prayed she wasn't blushing. "I miss you too."

Ryan's shoulders softened slightly. "You can't keep doing this."

"Doing what?"

He looked at her from the corner of his eye, his voice tender. "Are you ever going to tell me what's really going on with you?"

Cassie stared sightlessly out the windshield. "I did. I was walking home on the Powder River Trail, and it was dark, and I thought I heard something and my mind just..."

"Cassie, I saw the look on your face when you burst onto the street."

"I was spooked. Why can't you just let this go?" she bit back too quickly.

"Because it was more than that, and you know it."

He pulled into her long dirt driveway and came to a stop in front of her log cabin. Cassie didn't say a word because she couldn't, and that was always their problem.

She wanted to tell him everything. She wanted to tell him about her past, but it was against the rules, and in the Witness Protection Program, the rules were everything. After all, no witness who followed the rules had ever been killed in US Marshals' history. It was an impressive record. One that stilled her lips when her heart begged otherwise.

When she had first started dating Ryan, she'd believed her handler, Gerald Hawkins, would be on board with the relationship and let Ryan in on her situation. Unfortunately, the request had been firmly denied. It didn't matter that Ryan was a cop or that he was former FBI. Rules were rules, and who Ryan was and what he meant to her didn't matter. Cassie had pushed her handler to reconsider, but he opted to tell her sickening tales of what The Wolf would do to her if Ryan ever betrayed her.

"You can trust me. If…"

"Ryan, honestly," and she was being honest, "before I came to Bakerton, I was not in any abusive relationships."

"Then what is going on, Cassie?"

"Why are you always so suspicious? Can't I just be a girl scared by a stupid teenage prank?"

"Because there's more to this, and we both know it."

Their situation was impossible, and it didn't matter what she did. It wasn't going to get any better. Infuriated, Cassie hobbled out of the car and was surprised when she heard Ryan's door slam shut behind her. She turned. “I don’t want to fight.”

“I don’t want to fight either,” he said, holding up his hands in mock surrender. “I just want to make sure that the house is safe.”

Part of her wanted to say that she could take care of herself, but her throbbing knee strongly disagreed with her at the moment. “Knock yourself out,” she said, passing him the keys at the front door. He walked in first, and when she followed in behind him, he gave her a look. “It’s cold,” Cassie stated flatly. “I’m not waiting outside.”

He searched thoroughly around her sparsely furnished place. Not wanting to get caught staring after him, Cassie found herself overly focused on building a fire in the wood-burning stove.

“Everything appears fine,” he said, coming into the living room. “How’s your knee?”

“A little sore,” Cassie said, settling into the rocking chair and propping her leg up on the oversize ottoman.

Cautiously, he sat beside her knee. “Can I take a look?”

She thought about refusing, but it would only cause more problems if she didn’t let him. “Sure,” she said and drew up her torn pant leg. The knee was already starting to swell, and there were a couple of nasty scratches, but overall it didn't look too bad. His calloused hands tenderly touched her knee, making her heart quicken. He looked up from his examination, his eyes filled with gentleness.

So much was left unspoken between them, so much that begged to be said. The fire crackled, filling the silence.

"We should clean that up." Without another word, he disappeared into the kitchen. She heard him rummaging around her cupboards, banging things around.

"What are you doing in there?" she called.

"Looking for your kettle… It used to be… Found it… Hey, what do you think about me bringing Duke by and having him stay with you for a couple of days?"

"Duke? Sure. Are you going away?" Cassie asked, surprised. Ryan always took Duke, his golden Lab, with him everywhere when he wasn't on duty.

"No, just working a lot, and he always loved it out here. He'd be good company for you."

"Good protection, you mean."

"Something like that. What kind of tea do you want? You're out of peppermint."

"Chamomile would be perfect."

When he came back, Ryan had a tray laden

with snacks along with the tea. He set it beside her and brought a damp cloth up to her knee.

"I can take care of that," she said, tugging the cloth from his hand. Being near him was dangerous.

"There's an ice pack on the tray too. When you warm up a little, you should put it on."

"Will do."

He spied the TV remotes across the room and grabbed them for her. "I'll bring Duke by tomorrow morning. You should probably stay off that knee for a couple of days," he said, standing next to her Christmas tree.

"I'll try."

"Do more than try, okay?" He glanced over at her tree and his brow furrowed. Gently, he reached out, touching one of the ornaments they had made together last year.

"Are you staying for a bit?" Cassie asked.

"No. I need to get back," he said, pulling away.

Maybe she was a chicken, but she waited until he was behind her chair and opening the door before she asked what she needed to.

"Ryan…"

"Yeah?"

"Can I ask a favor?"

"Cassie, don't."

She twisted in her chair. “Please, don’t file a report about this.”

His words were icy as he turned his head away from her. “If you were just spooked, what does it matter?”

“Just don’t mention my name.”

Ryan shook his head. “I can’t believe you sometimes.”

“Ryan, please.”

“Good night, Cassie,” he said, shutting the door behind him with a decisive click.

Yet again, her heart was ripping into a million pieces. Ryan wanted to know everything about her, and that was something she couldn’t offer. Maybe their breaking up was for the best, but it didn’t make it easy. The headlights from his car shone through the entryway windows.

Cassie rose and walked to the bookshelf. Her fingers quickly tugged out an old copy of a novel and took the bookmark—a business card—out.

The white card contained simple black writing. *Gerald Hawkins—Tax Specialist* it read with a number listed below.

No longer crisp, the edges had become dog-eared and mired with smudges. Cassie had long since memorized the details, but she kept the card anyway. Sitting back down, she slowly twirled the paper between her fingers. Should she call her handler? she wondered.

The chances of the assassin—dubbed by the media as The Wolf—finding her were slim to none so long as she followed the rules of the program, and Cassie was nothing if not obedient. What were the odds that the person following her was The Wolf? Her fingers tapped the card.

It had been eight years since she had witnessed Congressman Johnson's assassination at the charity gala in her art studio in New York. Eight years since she'd testified against The Wolf's accomplice, Gabriel Finch, and it had been almost that long since the program had discouraged her from working publicly as an artist. In all the days and months that had passed since that awful night, The Wolf had yet to make a single attempt on her life. Not a single one.

Cassie didn't doubt that The Wolf still wanted her dead. After all, she had erased his anonymity. Her art skills had allowed her to make lifelike sketches and paintings of him and all that she had seen that night. The result had placed The Wolf's face on every major news network worldwide. With a stroke of her brush, she had made his face one of the world's most recognizable. And if that weren't enough, once he was caught, her testimony against The Wolf would ensure he was locked in prison for the rest of his life.

"What to do," Cassie muttered. Was the man on the trail tonight The Wolf or not? If it was The Wolf, wouldn't she be dead right now? She leaned back in her chair. Oddly, the thought gave her comfort.

Given her history, it was only natural that she would be skittish. She lifted the business card up, picturing Gerald, the kind, balding man who had become a good friend over the years.

If she told the program what happened tonight, Gerald might decide to relocate her. The thought hit likc a sucker punch to the gut. She'd already been stripped of her real family. The thought of returning to that nomadic lifestyle, of spending another Christmas alone, made her feel sick.

For the last three years, Bakerton had become Cassie's home. Here, she had joined a loving church and made friends who were more like family. This was her new beginning, and the thought of having it taken away for something that might be nothing was unthinkable.

With her mind made up, Cassie put the business card down. Her only hope was that Ryan wouldn't name her in a report if he filed one. If Gerald became aware of what happened tonight, her hands would be tied. He would present her with two options: relocate or quit witness protection. No matter how tough she had become, Cassie knew she wasn't ready to leave the safety the program afforded her.

She turned on the TV and found a baking show to distract her thoughts. There was no point in worrying about what Ryan would do. It had to rest in God's hands. She was safe, she was hidden, and no one, not even The Wolf, would be able to find her.

Ryan took a deep breath and parked his cruiser along the side of the snowbank where Cassie had burst into the intersection only an hour ago. As a former agent of the FBI, he was a master of staying calm underneath the most brutal of conditions, but seeing Cassie dart in front of his car the way she did had instantly stripped away his years of training. He hadn't run out of his car like an agent who had faced down serial killers. No, he'd acted like a lovesick schoolboy. While he'd left the FBI four years ago to become a small-town cop and live a simpler life, there still was no room for personal feelings to cloud his judgment.

Cassie was his ex-girlfriend for a reason.

Ryan didn't want to think of her mixed up in something illegal, but she was hiding something, and whatever that something was, she wanted him to overlook it. Unfortunately for her, his dad had taught him young the cost of being emotionally blinded.

Well, if he could put his own father behind bars, then he could do the same to her. He just needed to get his head in the game. What he needed were facts. Facts were tangible. Facts forced the truth, no matter how ugly, into the light.

Ryan got out of his warm car and pulled on his gloves. He didn't mind the cold tonight. The chill worked to center him and made his pulse slow. With his flashlight in hand, he easily picked up and followed Cassie's tracks, making him thankful the earlier snowfall had stopped.

Stepping up onto the Powder River Trail, Ryan observed the compacted snow where Cassie had stopped, turned and seen who was behind her. At that point, she had bolted through the trees. *Who had filled her with such terror?* Thankfully, with it being so late, the scene hadn't been contaminated by others. Ryan followed in his own footprints from before and counted off the distance from where Cassie had stood to where the perp's boot impressions had stopped. He looked up at the path light and noted that the man had been careful to remain on the edge of its reach. Not something the average teenage prankster would think to do.

Ryan bent down to study the assailant's tracks. He suspected they belonged to a man of medium height and medium build. He took pictures of the boot tread impression with his phone. Whoever this person was, they had stood in this spot, watched Cassie run and then doubled back. *Why didn't he chase after her?*

Puzzled, Ryan followed the footsteps back along the trail, noting when the man picked up his pace and how Cassie had tried to do the same. The snow made it simple to retell the story of what had unfolded.

Upon reaching the place of her original fall, Ryan traced back the perp's steps and found the spot where the man had stood in the trees. His jaw tightened when he shifted the evergreen branches revealing a perfect sight line to where Cassie had sat injured and vulnerable. He cleared his throat. A million different scenarios of what could have played out here tonight ran through his mind, and not one of them made the pit in his stomach feel any better.

He continued on to the entrance of Polson Park, where the streets had been plowed, obliterating the footprint trail. Since he knew Cassie's usual route, Ryan simply crossed the road. Her trail was easy to pick up, and so too were the tracks of the man that had followed her. Here Cassie's stride had been purposeful but didn't show signs of panic.

When he reached Cassie's Jeep, Ryan noticed a single half impression of the man's boot print behind it. From its angle, Ryan surmised the man must have crossed the street here. A few snow-encrusted cars dotted the far side of the road, but Ryan focused on the wide swaths of empty parking spots. Instinct told him that the perp had been parked somewhere along there, watching for a target or perhaps, waiting for a specific one. A tumult of conflicting emotions rose, and he quickly forced them down.

Ryan crossed Main Street and scanned for any evidence that someone had been loitering, but nothing turned up. Frustrated, he walked back to Cassie's Jeep and stood in front of it with his arms crossed over his chest. There had to be more here, he was sure of it. He stared carefully at the hood, now lightly covered in snow, and thought back on Cassie's story.

An idea began forming, and he squatted down to look through the grill, shining his flashlight. Ryan took his knife from his duty belt and maneuvered the blade, popping the hood. Methodically, he ran his flashlight over the engine and noticed the dirt was disturbed over the housing to the fuse box. His pulse racing, Ryan opened the housing, not wanting to see what he suspected.

But there it was, plain as day; one of the fuses had been pulled loose. Cassie's vehicle not starting had been no accident.

TWO

The clock over the television glared 2:32 a.m. Cassie stared at it disbelievingly. She should have gone to bed hours ago, but her mind would not stop replaying that unsettling whistle. Well, if she wasn't going to sleep, she might as well do something productive.

She hobbled toward the hall and made her way into the garage. Ignoring the chill, she slid into her blue Crocs and unlocked the door at the back of the space. If US Marshal Gerald Hawkins were to find out about this room, he would be furious with her, but in moments like this, Cassie was willing to face his wrath.

She flicked on the overhead fluorescent lights, her eyes squinting with the sudden bath of light over her art studio. The original owners had meant for the cement room to be storage, but from the moment Cassie had seen it, she'd known its potential. In fact, it was the main reason she had bought this cabin. It was her oasis. A place where she could safely paint without anyone noticing or figuring out who she was. Artwork, her fine arts professor had explained, was like a fingerprint, unique and identifiable to each artist. The last thing Cassie or WITSEC wanted was some well-meaning person to notice her talent and blow her cover by publicizing it.

Half asleep, Cassie took her old green sweater from its hook, wandered over to the easel and studied the canvas she was working on. In the past, she'd been drawn to modern artwork with intricate details. But since that fateful night at her gallery, she'd not had the heart for it. Now she dabbled in acrylics, letting herself drift into peaceful landscapes. The work proved challenging, and Cassie contemplated her current painting. Something was off with it. She tilted her head, studying the canvas. There it was. She had missed the reflection of light on some of the trees. By rote, she reached down for her fan brush, and her heart stilled.

She stared down in disbelief, her fingers rubbing against white velvety rose petals. Panic squeezed her chest. Cassie whirled around, sending her stool clattering onto the cement floor. She started to run and stopped short, her eyes glued to the open shelves next to the door. The disorganized chaos of water jars, paint thinners and artist materials now sat aligned in militant rows, but her eyes didn't register that. They only saw the painting. The landscape she'd completed last month now sat nailed into the wooden shelves, crude red lettering scrawled over the middle of it.

ordained with pure white roses,
their scent sweet upon your skin;
ardor long last requited,
love forever bound herein.

Holding her breath, Cassie reached forward and pushed her finger into the red paint. The acrylic, still tacky, stuck to her skin. She pressed her eyes closed, not wanting to believe the truth, but there it was, plain as the wet paint before her. A low scream tore from her throat as she ripped the canvas from the shelf and threw it across the room.

The Wolf had found her.

Fear and anger swirled together, threatening her focus, but Gerald's training began to take over her thoughts. She needed her go bag, and she needed to get out now. Without bothering to lock the door to her studio, Cassie ran to her bedroom.

Wrenching her packed black duffel from her

closet's top shelf, she threw it onto her bed. There was no time to waste. Quickly, Cassie opened her top drawer and leaped back. Her garments lay neatly in stacks, scattered with white rose petals. Her grandmother's necklace draped over the top of them. The violation tore at her gut, but she didn't have time to be afraid. With sure fingers, she snatched the locket from its perch and slammed the drawer shut.

A scratching sound echoed along the side of the house, and she jumped, looking over her shoulder. *It's just the maple tree.* Cassie steeled her heart and swiped her arm across the top of her dresser, scooping up the picture frames and shoving them into her bag.

A booming knock hammered at the front door. Cassie froze.

"I know you're up! I can see the lights."

Ryan? The banging came again, more insistent.

"Cassie, open up!"

She didn't have time for this right now.

Storming to the front door, Cassie threw it open. Duke bounded in, his wet front paws jumping up on her in his excitement to lick her face.

"Down, Duke," Cassie said authoritatively. The dog whined and nearly bowled her over, brushing against her legs, desperate for pets.

"Not now, Duke," she said, pushing him off and glowering at Ryan, who had shouldered his way past her with hands full of various pet paraphernalia. With a thump, Ryan dropped the giant bag of dog food on the kitchen counter.

"It's two in the morning?" Cassie stated, unable to keep the irritation out of her voice. "This couldn't wait?"

"No. It couldn't."

"Fine," she replied, gesturing him out the still-open front door. "Thanks for bringing Duke by. Good night."

Ryan squared his shoulders, matching Cassie's ruthless glare.

What on earth had gotten into him? Cassie pulled the door open a little wider, but Ryan didn't budge. From the hallway behind her, Duke pawed at her bedroom door, but she didn't dare break her stare down with Ryan.

"Leave it, Duke," Ryan said.

The dog whined and scratched again.

"Go lie down," Cassie said, not taking her eyes off Ryan. Duke's nails clicked on the floor as he made his way to the rug in front of the woodstove. The dog settled, letting out a deep harrumph, leaving no doubt to his displeasure with them.

Ryan crossed his arms over his chest. "I'm

not leaving until you tell me what really happened out there tonight."

Cassie let the door slam shut and swiftly closed the distance between them. Adrenaline coursing through her, she craned her neck to meet his eye and rose up on her tiptoes. Her retort was about to spill from her lips when she noticed the corded muscles in his neck. The glint in his eyes challenged her, but behind it, Cassie could now see the masked worry and how hard he was working to hide it from her.

This was all her fault. She stared up at the ceiling, inwardly counting to ten. "I already did. Look," she said calmly, "I'm tired. Can we talk about this some other time?"

"No, we can't. You're being targeted, and I want to know why."

"Targeted? I think you've watched too many *Castle* reruns," Cassie said, retreating into the living room.

"Someone watched you tonight, tampered with your Jeep and then stalked you through the woods." He gripped Cassie's shoulders and turned her to face him. "What would you call it?"

A flurry of emotions ran through her as his eyes searched her face. She pulled out of his grasp and sat down on the hearth, focusing all her attention on petting Duke. "Tampered with my Jeep?" she asked, trying to keep her voice sounding normal.

"Someone pulled the fuse loose so that it wouldn't start. Someone wanted you walking home tonight."

Duke sat up, leaning into the scratch behind his left ear. Deliberately, she kept focused on the dog. "It's the Christmas season, which means lots of tourists and the restaurant was busy. Sarah said a few customers seemed a little shady tonight. Maybe it was one of them."

Ryan sat down beside her, his arm innocently brushing against hers. "Maybe, but I don't think so."

Warmth flowed from him, eroding Cassie's defenses. How easy it would be to place her hand in his, to feel his arms wrap around her and lose herself in that feeling of security.

"Talk to me."

Cassie looked away, blinking back tears. "There's nothing for me to say."

"Please," he said, pushing Duke aside and sliding to his knees on the floor in front of her. His penetrating gaze begged her to relent. "Please trust me."

Cassie's heart flip-flopped in her chest. "Do we always have to come back to this?"

He shook his head, his cold eyes turning her stomach into a hard lump. He deserved better than this, but she couldn't provide the answers he wanted.

"You are hiding something. This is not in my head, Cassie," he said, standing up.

"What is that supposed to mean?"

"A normal person doesn't go to extreme lengths to make sure their restaurant isn't featured in the paper or reviewed," Ryan ranted. "A chef of your caliber should covet the attention that Mama Gina's is getting, but instead, you're threatening to close up shop. You claim to come from Ann Arbor, Michigan, yet you know nothing about its festivals, have never biked or hiked any of its world-class trails." He turned, pointing at her bookshelves. "You have no family pictures, photo albums or even mementos from past trips. There is nothing in this house that goes beyond your years in Bakerton. If I didn't know better, I'd ask if you're in WITSEC."

"What?" The shock at hearing him say the words registered on her face, and she played it to her advantage. "You're being ridiculous. I'm just a private person."

"It's more than that. You're hiding from someone, and from the terror I saw on your face earlier, I think that someone has come to Bakerton."

Lights of an approaching car shone through

the front hall window, causing Cassie to jump to her feet.

"It's Logan giving me a ride home. I brought your Jeep back. I didn't want you stranded out here."

Her pulse slowed. "Thank you. That was thoughtful." Cassie's brow furrowed. "Wait, how'd you get the key?"

"I remembered that you gave Sarah a spare set for when she runs restaurant deliveries."

"You woke up Sarah for this? It's two in the morning."

"Sarah's not just some employee working at your restaurant. She's your best friend and trust me, she didn't mind. I needed to talk to her about what happened tonight." His tone gentled. "She's worried about you."

"Ryan!" Cassie cried.

He stepped closer, ignoring her outrage, and tenderly took her hands in his. "Look, if you're mixed up in something, if you've done something…"

"Done something?" Cassie shoved off his hands. "Done something? You think I'm a criminal?"

"Then file a complaint about what happened tonight," he challenged.

This was a nightmare. Cassie turned her back on him, staring at the painted wood paneling, unseeing. He didn't understand what he was asking of her. He didn't understand that putting her name on that report symbolized her never speaking to or seeing anyone from this town ever again. Cassie closed her eyes, pressing back the tears. But at this point, what did it matter? The Wolf had found her. She was leaving Bakerton tonight and never coming back.

He stood over her shoulder, his tone pleading. "If some man is pulling fuses from women's cars, stalking them in the trees, you need to file a report."

"Ryan…"

"I know you, Cassie. The only reason that you are refusing me is because you know that no one else is at risk."

Cassie faced him.

"And you know no one is at risk," he continued, "because you know who was out there, and you know that you're who they want. That is the only reason the Cassie I know wouldn't file a report."

"Fine," she said, staring into his disbelieving eyes, "I'll file a report."

"What?"

"If you'll let me get some sleep, I'll come to your office in the morning and give a statement. File an official report."

Ryan looked at her skeptically. "You'd do that?"

"Like you said, if someone else is at risk, then I have to. Right?" Her eyes burned from holding back the tears. As soon as he was out of sight, she'd take off for the extraction point that Gerald had set up for occasions like this. It tore at her heart that these heated words would be the last they ever exchanged. This was not how she wanted their relationship to end. Taking a deep breath, Cassie allowed the weariness she felt to show. "Look, I'm sore and tired. This has been a really long night."

"You'll come in tomorrow morning?"

"Yes," she said. "Look, I appreciate everything you've done, but I would really like to get some sleep." Cassie walked over to the front door and pulled it open. "Good night, Ryan."

The radio from Ryan's police vest squelched to life. "Ryan, we got a report of a 12-45."

"Copy that, on my way," Ryan said, answering Logan.

Duke raised his head from where he'd flopped on the rug and stared at them.

There was nothing more Ryan could say. She could tell he didn't trust her, but other than arresting her, what more could he do? Her request was reasonable, given the situation.

"In the morning then. Good night, Cassie," Ryan said with a tip of his hat at the front door.

"Good night, Ryan."

Cassie waited for Logan to pull out of the driveway before disappearing down the hall to get her bag. Her heated words with Ryan began replaying in her mind, and she pushed the thoughts back. If she wanted to live, she needed to concentrate on getting out of here.

It only took one step into her bedroom to realize something was wrong. Cassie inhaled sharply as the heat clicked on, making the drapes billow. The window was open, the screen torn out and a thin dusting of snow now glimmered in the moonlight on the hardwood floor. Cassie's heartbeat hammered against her ribs, her eyes scanning the room. Nothing seemed displaced. Her black duffel bag sat in the middle of her white bedspread, the closet door was still askew from her earlier rush and the books on her nightstand lay undisturbed. All she had to do was dash in, grab the bag and go. It was a simple task.

Simple and yet Cassie's feet remained rooted to the floor. Her eyes clung to the black duffel with over fifty thousand dollars in it. The edges of the lace bed skirt swayed gently with the winter breeze.

"Duke!" Cassie yelled, retreating to the front door, "Duke, come!"

It was hard to let the money go, but she had a second bag stashed at the restaurant. Gerald had always been adamant that she have a plan B, and now she was thankful for it.

Duke barked and followed her out the door, leaping into the Jeep after her.

"Just one quick stop at the restaurant, and then I'll drop you off at home," Cassie said, giving him a quick scratch and then gunning the engine.

Ryan put his hands on either side of his kitchen sink and stared out the window. The night felt alive, its shadows doing nothing to calm his nerves. Something was out there. He could sense it in the marrow of his bones. Whatever it was, the five-foot chain-link fence surrounding his yard wasn't going to guard against it.

"Everything downstairs looks fine to me," Logan said, entering the kitchen behind him.

"You could have said the 12-45 was an alarm at my house," Ryan bit out, not taking his gaze from the window. "Instead of parking one block up and explaining the situation while we snuck up on my place."

"If you would have let me get a word in, instead of blathering on about Cassie and your latest conspiracy theory about her, maybe I would have. Besides, it wouldn't have changed the plan," Logan said, unperturbed as Ryan glared at him. Stretching his tall frame, Logan stifled a yawn and found his place at the wooden breakfast table in the small kitchen lit only by the light over the stove. "Nothing's been disturbed or taken from your place. This whole call was probably just some kids playing a prank."

The word *prank* rankled Ryan, doing nothing to improve his mood. "My gut disagrees with you."

"You forget who you're talking to?" Logan asked, raising his dark bushy eyebrows. "That gut of yours has led us astray more than once over the years, and I've got the scars to prove it. Now, as your boss, I've got to say there's nothing wrong here, and we'd best get back to work. As your best friend, what is up with you?"

"I don't know what you're talking about," Ryan said, sparing a glance over his shoulder.

"You gonna make me say it? I'll say it," Logan said, resting his forearms casually on the table.

Ryan's eyes narrowed. "Don't go there."

"Someone has to. Cassie was the best thing

that ever happened to you, and not only did you mess it up, but it's like you go out of your way to continue making things worse."

"I don't want to have this conversation."

"Tough. Someone needs to set you straight."

"And you think three thirty in the morning is the time to do it?"

"If the moment's right, it's right. You and she were inseparable, the perfect fit. Which is something that I never believed existed until I saw the two of you together." Logan took his hat from his head and flopped it on the table. "You even brought her fly-fishing with us, and in fifteen years, we've *never* brought anyone—not even my brother—fishing with us. I don't understand how you can walk away from someone like that."

"Because she's lying," Ryan spat out. Of all people, he shouldn't have to explain this to Logan. His best friend should have his back.

"We searched every database we have access to and called in favors to search the ones we don't," Logan said, tapping the table with his forefinger to emphasize his next words. "Cassie has never committed a crime."

"Or she just hasn't been caught."

"Think about who you're talking about. Cassie teaches Sunday school, started up the benevolent meals program at our church and while her singing voice may be more akin to a crow than a canary, I don't think that's reason enough to lock her up. Exactly what do you think she's guilty of?"

"I don't know," Ryan admitted. "But I can't be with someone who's holding out on me."

Logan sighed. "For argument's sake, let's say she did do something. You don't know what or why she did it. Maybe it's not that bad."

Ryan raised one eyebrow. "Or maybe it's worse."

"I think you're way off base on this one. There's no way the Cassie I know is mixed up in anything illegal."

With everything that had gone on tonight, it was hard for Ryan to bite his tongue. But there was no point in arguing. He and Logan were never going to see eye to eye on this.

"You're going to leave Bakerton because of her, aren't you?"

Dumbfounded, Ryan shook his head. "Why would you say that?"

"Your old boss at the FBI called me again yesterday. He said the two of you have been talking."

Ryan winced.

"Walter wants you back on his team. You're a good agent with an impressive arrest record, so I can see why. And with the way things are between you and Cassie," Logan looked at Ryan supportively, "a change in scenery might be nice."

"It's not that simple."

"Maybe it is. No one is arguing that you had some tough cases before you left the FBI. It even made sense that you came here to get away for a bit, but it has been four years. Buddy, everyone is wondering, are you going back to work for them?"

"I haven't decided."

A loud bark came from the backyard, grabbing Ryan's attention and drawing Logan to his back.

"I thought Duke..."

"He is," Ryan said, cocking his gun and ripping open the sliding glass door. He stepped onto the back deck but deliberately left the porch light off. He could just make out a figure kneeling near Duke's doghouse. "Who's there?" he called out, his pulse rising when the person rose to their feet. Cassie. He knew it before she even spoke a word. He'd know her anywhere.

"It's me," Cassie confirmed, holding up her arms in surrender. "No need to bring out the artillery."

"I could have shot you," Ryan said, holstering his gun and moving to the edge of the porch.

"I didn't think you were home," she said.

"Cassie?" Logan said, emerging from the house. "What're you doing here?"

"I'll tell you what she's doing." Ryan's fingers strangled the metal railing, the snow turning to liquid under his bare palm. "She's running. Aren't you?"

"Of course that's what you'd think," Cassie spit out. "I'm not sticking around for this." She turned and walked across the yard, heading for the gate on the side of the house.

He knew it wasn't rational, but something in his gut told him that once she went through that gate, he would never see her again. Sick with emotions he couldn't name, Ryan took the porch stairs two at a time. "Only guilty people run," he yelled, stopping not far behind her.

Cassie paused.

Hope soared in his hollow chest, and Ryan didn't even think to squelch it. Instead, he braved a cautious step forward. "Please, stay," he said.

The night stretched silently between them.

"It's not that simple," she finally answered, her voice tight, "it's just not." And with that, she hurried toward the gate.

Her words ignited a storm within him. Vivid

memories from his past boiled up. He could almost see his dad's scrawny frame opening the apartment door, both of them knowing the police were on the way. *It's never that simple, son*, was all that man had said before leaving. His own father hadn't cared what happened to him and, for that matter, never would.

Ryan's fingers bit into Cassie's puffer jacket and spun her around.

"Just tell me what you've done," he growled into her shocked face.

"What are you talking about?"

"I can't picture you as a drug dealer or a murderer, I've tried, but I can't. So what are you? A con artist? Is that who's chasing you? Some poor victim wanting revenge?"

Cassie pushed hard at his chest, hurt flaring in her eyes. He let her go, and at the sudden release, she stumbled backward. "You're going to wake your neighbor if you keep up with all this yelling."

"I'll figure it out," he snapped as Logan rushed down the squeaky porch steps. "Trust me. You're in a database somewhere."

"How can you…how can you think…"

Duke snarled, and Ryan turned just in time to see movement from the woods. Instinctually, he pulled Cassie behind him when the back steps exploded, and Logan was catapulted forward toward a low retaining wall at the back of the yard. A guttural cry escaped from Logan's lips as a short piece of metal railing lodged in his leg.

The fence rattled hard as Duke hurled himself at the panel, his lead holding him back.

"Verbergen!" Ryan yelled, using the German command for his dog to hide. Instantly, his FBI training took over, moving Ryan's emotions into a box for later. He pushed Cassie and himself behind the garden shed and smoothly drew his gun. Peering around the corner, he leaned out when an answering hail of bullets pinged off the metal above their heads.

He drew Cassie down into a low crouch beside him, shielding her with his body until the bullets stopped. "Keep low," he said, switching off his police radio.

"What are you doing?"

"There could be more explosives, and I can't risk setting them off," Ryan said, taking a deep breath. "No cell phones, no radio frequencies within one hundred yards. It's protocol."

"Tell me you're kidding."

"I wish that I were." His hand squeezed hers. Until tonight, he'd loved living on the edge of the woods. "The Bannisters are good neighbors. They'll call this in."

"They're your only neighbors down here,"

she said, her face turning thoughtful. "And I think Sarah mentioned they were leaving for Seattle to visit their daughter for Christmas?"

"Let's hope you heard wrong," he said and dared another look around the corner of the shed.

The explosion had been a small one, with structural damage limited to the back steps and porch. While the house remained virtually unscathed, Logan had not been so fortunate. His best friend lay on the ground, groaning as he pulled himself toward the retaining wall, attempting to gain protective cover. Logan's hand stretched forward, and a shot sliced through his palm.

Ryan fought the urge to run to his friend. An action that would surely get them both killed. Instead, he carefully analyzed the tree line. No movement.

"I can cover you," Cassie said.

"What?" Ryan replied, half listening while he peeked around the corner of the shed. Where was this guy perched? His eyes scoured the dense tree line when an all too familiar clicking sound came from behind him. He glanced over, shocked to see Cassie on the far side of the shed with her back to it and a Glock 20 in her hands, ready to go. "What do you think you're doing?"

"I can shoot better than you and Logan at the range and I've watched the two of you practice training scenarios together." She met his eyes with bold confidence. "I'll cover you," she repeated.

"I can't let you do that. You're not an officer, you don't have the proper training and we don't have a visual on the assailant. Put that away."

"There is a lot about me that you don't know," she said, her eyes narrowing. "And I do have a line of sight. I got it when he shot Logan in the hand."

Ryan didn't have time for arguments. He peered around the edge of the shed, his mind grappling for a plan. How long would it take for backup to get out here? He glanced at his watch. If help had indeed been called, it would take them a while to assemble and mobilize. He listened for sirens but heard nothing.

Cassie moved next to him. "I can't carry Logan to safety, but you can."

"Are you out of your mind?" he said. There was no way he could allow her to discharge a weapon right now. It would violate every police directive known to man.

Logan let out a pain-filled groan that drew Ryan's attention back to the scene. His friend lay motionless on the ground, a dark bloom of red staining the snow around him. Ryan's heart plummeted into his stomach. He had to do something. Logan couldn't take another hit.

"Come with me," Cassie said, leading Ryan to the opposite corner of the shed. "There's muzzle flash at one o'clock, approximately fifty yards from us. You don't like this, I get it, but I'm all you've got right now. I know what I'm doing."

Ryan found the spot Cassie had indicated but saw no betraying movement from the assailant. Before he could stop her, Cassie took the hat off his head and threw it out beside the shed. Bullets cracked into the night, and like she had promised, he spotted the muzzle flash from beside a tree.

"You could get all of us killed," Ryan said, his stomach sinking.

"If we do nothing, we all get killed too."

Ryan turned, his thoughts reeling. His ears strained to hear sirens, any indication that help was on the way, but again he heard nothing. He stalked back to the other side of the shed and stared at Logan. A bullet narrowly missed his friend's head. As much as Ryan didn't like her plan, Cassie was a crack shot and there were no other options. He met Cassie's eyes. "Are you sure you can handle this?"

"I would never risk Logan or you if I wasn't."

He searched her face but already knew

she was telling the truth. Ryan said a silent prayer, not liking anything about this situation. "Okay," he relented, his stomach twisting. "You've practiced with Logan and me." He studied her carefully, looking for any sign of hesitation. "Do you remember how this goes?"

Cassie nodded and took a few steps back from the shed, angling to get the best shot and maintain good cover. "On go," she said, finding her firing stance and carefully aiming. "Ready," Cassie called, her eyes locked on their target.

"Ready."

"Go," she said and began shooting at the assailant.

Ryan kept low across the snow and reached Logan's side in seconds. "It's me, buddy," he said, rolling Logan from his side onto his back.

His friend let out a pain-filled grunt and met Ryan's eye. "So I think you're right."

"What's that?"

"Cassie's definitely mixed up in something."

Ryan choked on a laugh. "Glad we can finally agree on it," he said, turning his attention back to the gunfight going on above their heads. Cassie had the gunman busy, but there wasn't much time. He grabbed Logan's shoulders and dragged his friend toward the shed, out of the line of fire. Once they reached safety,

Ryan ripped open the Velcro pouch on Logan's police vest that held his individual first aid kit. Pulling out the black strap tourniquet, he slid it under Logan's leg. "Sorry about this," he said and cinched the tourniquet tight as Logan emitted an ear-piercing screech.

Shots peppered the shed, and Ryan leaned over Logan protectively. "I need to bandage your hand. Are you hit anywhere else?"

"I don't think so," Logan said, his breathing tight from fighting back the pain.

Sirens blared in the distance, and Ryan thanked God under his breath. "Hang in there, okay?" he said, wrapping the hand wound.

He patted down Logan's body looking for other injuries, when he realized the gunfire had stopped. His heart clenched. Cassie. He looked over his shoulder and saw her sitting huddled against the far side of the shed. She met his gaze and gave him the okay sign, and he found himself able to breathe again.

"What's going on over there?" he called to Cassie.

"The guy ran when the sirens started. I lost sight of him in the woods. How's Logan?"

"Been better," Logan said through gritted teeth. "But I'll live."

"Cassie, can you come over here and give me a hand?" Instantly, Cassie slid over, holstering her gun. She looked so calm and cool that he couldn't help but wonder who this woman was. He met her eyes over Logan's body and shoved his thoughts aside. "We need to get Duke and us away from my house in case it blows. Can you help me get Logan across the street?"

"Definitely."

"Hier," Ryan yelled, calling Duke to his side. The dog appeared and eagerly tried to lick Ryan's face when he removed Duke's lead. This was one of the many reasons that Duke hadn't been successful in the K-9 program.

Together the three of them and Duke made their way through the gate and hurried across the road. In perfect unison, Cassie and Ryan lowered Logan to the ground behind two large boulders that served as a trailhead marker. Logan's face looked pale, but the sirens were getting closer. Help would be here any minute.

Ryan sensed more than saw Cassie look toward her Jeep. It sat parked on the side of the road, not far from them.

"Don't do it," Ryan said, checking Logan's tourniquet to make sure it hadn't loosened in the transfer.

"I have to," she said and ran for her vehicle.

Ryan's thoughts turned thunderous. What was he supposed to do? He couldn't leave Logan and chase her down.

Logan gripped his hand. “Go after her.”

“I won’t leave you.”

“Help is almost here.” Logan lifted his right hand and wobbled his gun. “I’ll be fine until they get here, but she’ll be long gone by then. *Go!*”

Ryan hesitated.

“I’m your boss, and I’m giving you an order. Whoever was out there could easily have killed me tonight but didn’t, and I want to know why. This isn’t just about you anymore. Go get her.”

Logan had a point, but Cassie had a head start.

“*Such* Cassie,” Ryan said, the single command sending Duke racing down the road. Duke reached her in seconds and playfully jumped all around her, blocking Cassie from getting any closer to the driver’s door. His dog might not be ferocious, but he was very effective.

“Call him off!”

“When the party gets here,” Ryan said, referring to the emergency vehicles that were getting closer. “You have some explaining to do.”

“I don’t have time for that.” Cassie turned and faced the dog. “Duke, sit.”

Duke complied, squirming with the hope of reward. “Good boy.” Cassie sidestepped the animal and got in the vehicle.

Ryan's eyes narrowed. If she thought she was getting away that easily, she had another thing coming. He sprinted for the Jeep and yanked open the passenger door, hopping in the seat before she could bolt.

"Take us to the station."

Duke barked from behind the vehicle, and Cassie waited for Ryan to let the dog in.

"Not this time," she said and floored the accelerator.

THREE

Ryan rubbed his brow and felt Logan's blood smear across his forehead. Undeterred by anything, Cassie sped them across the town line, away from police and away from any help. His hands dropped onto his lap. His eyes transfixed to the bright red rivulets that were turning dark and hardening in the creases of his skin. He forced himself to look away. An innocent person did not run.

Cassie met his eyes when she switched gears, making his breath catch. When she looked at him like that, it made him want to believe things that contradicted the situation they were now in and why they were in it. He noticed the exhaustion tugging at the edges of her eyes, her tight grip on the steering wheel. She was starting to fall apart.

Deliberately, he bent his fingers and felt Logan's dried blood buckling on his skin. His gut twisted. Cassie was not innocent, and it was best he did not forget that.

Knowing what he had to do, Ryan reached into his pocket, but his fingers faltered when they touched the hard plastic case of his cell phone. He needed to phone in their location. He should have done it the moment he got into Cassie's Jeep, but something made him pause.

"I'm sorry about Logan. Do you think he'll be okay?" she asked, daring another glance at him.

"He'll survive. Not that you stuck around to find out."

The hurt in her eyes gnawed at his gut, and he instantly regretted the words. Her head snapped back to the road, but she said nothing in response. She sat tall, her long auburn locks cascading over the line of her shoulders. He wanted to comfort her, to look down at her freckled nose and tell her it would all be okay.

A car driving by left their high beams on, making him wince and look down. His jacket was stained with Logan's blood. What was he thinking? She was responsible for what had happened to Logan. She was just like his dad—all smiles and charm, but when the dust settled, it always turned out to be lies and illusions. The reality of it hurt, but at least the hurt was real.

He took a deep breath, pulled the phone from his pocket and began to dial in the number.

"What are you doing?"

"I'm letting them know where we are. This is Officer Matherson…"

Cassie glared. "Hang up."

"Please patch me through to…"

Cassie grabbed for his phone as the Jeep caught an edge of black ice. The vehicle slid toward the rock face and then swung into a rear tailspin across the road. Duke howled. Ryan's head cracked into the passenger window, his phone flying out of his hands. The Jeep swung erratically and then, abruptly, everything came to a standstill.

With a whimper, Duke leaped into Ryan's lap. It was all fur and tail in his face as the dog performed an awkward pirouette. Finally, Duke settled his body uncomfortably across the two of them, his head and front paws hanging over Cassie's armrest. She leaned down and soothingly stroked the dog's head. Duke wormed closer to her while digging his back claws into Ryan's thigh, making Ryan grit his teeth.

Quiet fell over the Jeep as crisp white snowflakes fell on the windshield. Two straight beams from their headlights cut a path through the predawn darkness, revealing the cliff and valley on the other side of the road. Things could be a whole lot worse right now.

"Officer Matherson, are you there? Is everything okay, Officer Matherson?" came the muffled voice from the cell phone.

Cassie's hand rested lightly on his forearm. He looked into those vulnerable eyes, and his heart lurched. He lifted the phone from the floor and put it to his ear. "I'll have to call you back."

"Thank you," Cassie whispered as he hung up.

Ryan's cell immediately rang, and he switched it off. Was he making a mistake? He eyed her suspiciously. The one thing he had learned from his dad was how to sniff out a lie. The real question was, could he be objective where Cassie was concerned?

"I expect answers," he said flatly.

"I know you do," Cassie replied, coaxing Duke into the back seat. The dog groaned but was exhausted enough that he cooperated.

"Now," Ryan snarled, his patience wearing thin.

"You have to understand. This conversation violates the rules."

"You tell me now, or I call my boys in blue and tell them to come and get us."

Cassie slipped the gearshift into first. "Fine," she agreed, but instead of talking, she began praying.

Her words fell softly from her lips, provoking a strong desire for him to take her hand in his.

Appalled, Ryan shook his head. "Stop it. Stop it right now." He didn't have time for this. He needed answers. Ryan held up his phone. "I'm not joking. You either start talking or I start phoning." His finger edged toward the power button on his cell. Every part of him wanted to press it, but a little voice in the back of his head kept telling him to be patient.

I'm done being patient, Ryan wanted to yell. She was manipulating him. Couldn't God see that?

Cassie looked at him from the corner of her eye and then focused on the road.

She took a deep breath. "You remember when Congressman Johnson was murdered a few years ago at a fundraising art gala?"

"Yeah."

"And there was also an artist, Cassandra Roberts, who witnessed the hit… She made sketches and paintings of everything she'd seen."

Ryan rolled his eyes. "The first and only person to put a face to the assassin known as

The Wolf," Ryan said, unable to hide the irritation in his voice as he recited the tagline that followed Cassandra Roberts's name on news cycles. "I think the whole world knows about her."

The media coverage of the assassination had reached such a global fervor that even now, eight years later, Congressman Johnson, Cassandra Roberts and The Wolf were household names. The fact that the case had never been solved only added to its allure. While the investigation into the congressman's death hadn't been his case when he was at the Bureau, he was familiar with the facts and was well aware that several FBI teams were still investigating the case.

"Then you know that even with her sketches out there, law enforcement has never caught The Wolf and the person who hired him was never identified."

"Yes," Ryan said, his jaw beginning to clench. He didn't like where this was going. Chances were she was about to tell him a whopper of a lie, but then again, he couldn't ignore how she handled herself with a gun. Cassie's marksmanship wasn't a skill someone just picked up. That was something that took years of practice. He'd imagined her as a lot of things over the last few months, but never someone mixed up with an assassination. He shifted in his seat. Could she have helped the hit man that night? It was hard to believe. Then again, he'd run her name through the government databases, and that Glock wasn't registered to her.

Was any part of that kind, loving person he'd known genuine? He closed his eyes, steeling his gut to the truth. The Cassie he thought he'd known wasn't real. None of their time together was. That's how criminals worked. They created an illusion that provided what you longed for to prevent you from seeing the con.

He tried to control his voice, but a bite still clung to his words. "So, you're telling me you were somehow involved the night of the congressman's death?"

"Yes."

"How?"

Her teeth nibbled her lower lip. "I'm the artist. I'm Cassandra Roberts."

Ryan couldn't hide his disbelief. "Cassie, you don't look anything like her. I'm not stupid. Her face was in every news cycle around the world for months."

"I know I don't look like her," she said, sparing him a pleading glance, "but I am being honest with you."

Ryan picked up his phone.

"You need to hear me out." Cassie took another deep breath. "Being accepted into the witness protection program isn't easy. I went through three separate psychological assessments, but that still didn't prepare me for what was to come. As you said, my face was plastered all over the news and everywhere I went, people kept recognizing me. So, the US Marshals moved me into heavy seclusion and kept me there for years. I'm not proud of it, but I ended up spiraling into a depression. We all knew I couldn't keep going on like I was, but what other options were there? The congressman's death had been an international media circus. That's when the idea of plastic surgery came up."

"The Marshals don't do that. That's the stuff of spy novels."

Cassie ignored him. "Again, there was another round of brutal psychological assessments. Picture me with a different nose and short black hair."

"I'm calling in."

"Honest, Ryan, I'm Cassandra Roberts. I'm the artist. I've been in Witness Protection for the last eight years."

Ryan rolled his eyes. This was getting comical.

"I'm not lying. I can prove it. Grab my duffel bag."

He stared at her, unmoving.

"Just do it."

Ryan leaned into the back, shoving Duke out of the way, and pulled the heavy bag onto his lap. He unzipped the main compartment and found it half-stuffed with hundred-dollar bills and clothes.

"Whoa, this is a lot of cash! What are you doing with all of this?"

"Comes in handy when you're on the run. Look in the pockets on the side of the bag."

Ryan followed her instructions and pulled out a small packet. He undid the battered string and began leafing through old family photos. The pictures were definitely of a young Cassandra Roberts. He couldn't dispute that, nor the auburn hair that she sported. The girl stood at different ages with people he assumed were her relatives. The last was of Cassandra Roberts in her twenties, her hair short and dark, with someone he'd guess was her grandpa standing before a large modern painting.

He sat quietly. "WITSEC wouldn't let Cassandra keep photos like this."

"They were well hidden."

Ryan flipped through the photos again and paused on the one with her and her grandfather. He held it up, looking at her and then at the picture.

The morning light was beginning to burn through the darkness, making Cassie's fiery hair come alive with a soft glow. His breath caught in his chest. Even now, he had to admit she was the most beautiful woman he had ever met. He shook his head. Slowly, his eyes traced over her face, comparing her to the photograph. The eyes were the same sparkling hazel, and her left cheek held the same small dimple when she smiled. His gaze dropped to her lips and lingered; they both had the same full shape.

Cassie's head turned shyly away. "The pixie cut was really in back then," she said too quickly. "And the black hair was an artsy thing at the time."

Could it be true? Or was the likeness his wishful thinking?

"I'm surprised they let you do the surgery?" he said, putting the photos back in their envelope, his voice softer.

"Trust me. It was a last resort."

"You could have gotten these pictures many different ways, and a bag of cash doesn't tell me anything," he commented, his voice lacking enthusiasm.

"But my memories will."

He turned silent, focusing his eyes on the passing landscape.

"You worked for the Bureau. Let me tell you

about that night, and you'll know I'm telling the truth."

"Cassie."

"It's the only way you'll believe me."

"I don't know about this."

"All I'm asking is that you listen," she said, plunging ahead. "My manager's name was Sylvia Dubois, and to show off my latest art installation, we were hosting a charity gala. It was supposed to be small. She was supposed to limit the number of invitations, but Sylvia found it hard to turn away potential clients." Cassie let out a bemused sigh. "I should have known when she insisted on a string quartet that it was going to be bigger than I wanted."

"String quartet? It sounds like it was quite the event."

"It was," Cassie said, lost in thought. "Sylvia never missed a beat. But all those people." Cassie wrinkled her nose.

"Crowds are not your thing."

Cassie nodded. "To this day, when I hear 'Silent Night,' I feel claustrophobic. All those people in my gallery, it was hot and I was wearing this blue velvet dress that didn't breathe." Her voice caught in her chest. "I just needed to get out of there, even if it was just for five minutes. I was about to sneak away when Sylvia caught me trying to escape."

Ryan shook his head. "Cassie, I'm struggling to buy this." The words were lining up with what he knew, but something was off. "None of it sounds like you. Crowded galas, string quartets, velvet dresses—it's all too fussy. And I can't imagine you working with someone you had to escape from. Sylvia sounds like a tyrant."

"It was a very different life." A smile tipped the corners of Cassie's mouth. "And Sylvia wasn't a tyrant. She was more my protector. You see, the congressman wanted to meet me, and one of my important clients, Elaine Baccara, was trying to impress him by facilitating it. Sylvia realized I wasn't up for it and ran interference, allowing me to disappear into my bunker."

"Bunker?" Ryan raised an eyebrow, knowing that the term had not made the news cycles.

"That's what Sylvia called my studio because it was in the basement, under the gallery. The lighting system down there was state-of-the-art, but it was stark and cement. In a lot of ways, it looked like a bunker, but I loved it there. It gave me the privacy I needed while still being close to the gallery."

"A sanctuary of sorts."

"It was, just not that night." Cassie nibbled her lip. "That dress was like a torture device, and I was so hot. I went out into the basement stairwell." Cassie paused. "You know, if I smell damp cement, it still brings me back to that moment." She shivered.

Ryan wanted to reach out to her but forced himself to remain still.

"I went to go back in when I heard a car pull into the alley and park, leaving its motor running. The congressman and his security man, Gabriel, came outside. They were arguing because the congressman didn't want to leave." Cassie looked at Ryan sheepishly. "Hearing the congressman's voice, I was curious and stood on my tiptoes to peek above the cement rise. Sometimes I wonder what my life would have been like if I hadn't done that. If I'd just gone back inside."

"*What if* is an awful game to play," Ryan said, feeling himself shifting into believing her. "Coming forward, using your artistic talents the way you did, that was brave."

"I don't regret that. I don't," she said, pulling her eyes away from the road. "It's just sometimes I wonder what would have happened if I never had the gala, or if..."

"Cassie," Ryan said, putting his hand on her shoulder. "You can't go down that road."

She shrugged off his touch and stared at the highway. A tear welled in the corner of her eye, and Cassie swiped it away. "When I think about that night, I can still see it, like it's happening all over again. The congressman tried to push past Gabriel, tried to phone someone, but then it all went sideways. Gabriel pulled a gun, and at first, I thought the congressman was going to cooperate and get in the car, but instead, he lunged for the gun. Then I heard the town car door shut…" Cassie gulped for air as she tried to push back the tears. "I felt paralyzed. I couldn't take my eyes from the driver's face. I just stood there while he…"

Ryan rubbed her arm soothingly. "You don't need to tell me anymore. I believe you."

FOUR

Seeing the large yellow sign with flickering red letters advertising the Ludlow Motel just outside of Hermiston, Oregon, Cassie slowed and turned into the near-empty parking lot. It had been over two hours since they had left Bakerton, but for Cassie's exhausted body, it felt like the drive had taken twenty.

The squat two-story building, a mixture of red siding and dingy white stucco, sat sadly along the side of the highway. Its aged yellow sign forever hoping to lure travelers with its promise of affordable holiday pricing and HBO. It hadn't gotten any prettier since the last time she'd been here. Pulling into a parking spot next to the office, Cassie yawned. Her eyelids felt so heavy that she was afraid if she blinked too long, she'd fall asleep.

Ryan leaned across her and looked out the driver's side window, his nose wrinkled. "This is what the US Marshals are using for safe houses these days?"

"It's not a safe house." She looked at Ryan and tried to think how to explain this. "I'm not a trained agent, so if something goes sideways and I'm forced to run, the Marshals want me to focus on getting away and staying alive. Their computers monitor police reports in Bakerton, so if I'm involved in any incident they are automatically alerted. To increase my chances of survival they've scouted out several different places near Bakerton that I'm to head to when in trouble. They're spots they consider a good place to lie low until they can get to me," she said sensibly. "Basically, they've simplified where I'm to hide and where to start their search." Cassie stared at the ugly motel. "I'm sure the FBI has used worse locations to meet people."

He shifted, his eyes crinkling at the edges as he examined her face. "Not for someone like you," he said.

Her heart skittered. Ryan's blue eyes stared into hers with such sincerity; it felt like the world was tilting. *Don't be ridiculous*, Cassie admonished herself silently. He doesn't mean anything by those words. She forced a smile onto her lips and playfully pushed him back toward his seat, trying to ignore the heat rising in her cheeks.

Cassie stepped out of the vehicle and took a deep breath of the brisk morning air.

The Jeep door shut behind her. She spun on her heel to see Ryan standing on the far side of it. “Where do you think you’re going?”

“In there,” he said, exaggeratedly pointing to the office door, “with you.”

“I don’t think so.”

“And why not?”

She swirled her finger at his uniform. “I think they’ll take cash under the table a lot easier from someone not dressed in a blood-covered uniform.”

Ryan let out an undignified snort. “Cash under the table? How cheap are these marshals?”

“Just stay in the Jeep,” she said, tossing him the keys. Cassie crossed the parking lot and felt his eyes glued to her back. She wasn’t sure whether that was a good thing or not. Over the last couple of hours, things between them had changed, but she wasn’t sure what that meant for either of them.

The chime over the door rang when she walked inside the square box of an office. Instantly, the smell of mildew and cigarettes assailed her nostrils. Cassie wrinkled her nose, her eyes adjusting to the dark space. Someone had tried to inject some Christmas cheer into the room by taping a red plastic poinsettia garland to the walls and shoving an inflatable snowman into the corner. It was a valiant effort. Cassie placed a smile on her face, marched up to the high wood counter and waited for someone to appear.

"Hello?" she called, but the only sound came from the hum of the inflatable in the corner.

When no one appeared, Cassie gave in and rang the bell. A chair groaned from a room off to the side, and a young man with curly blond hair appeared through the open doorway. His plastic Ludlow Motel tag announced his name as Crawford.

"How can I help you?" he said, brushing crumbs off his wrinkled, button-down shirt.

"I need two adjoining rooms, please."

The chunky keys of his historic computer clacked. "How many people will be staying with us?"

"Just me and a friend for two nights."

"I'll need to see some ID and a credit card to secure the room."

"How about I pay in cash, and we forget about the ID and credit card."

He looked up from his computer, a bored sigh escaping his lips. "Ma'am, what kind of establishment do you think this is?"

Cassie reached into her pocket, pulled out four hundred-dollar bills and placed them side by side on the counter. "One that doesn't judge. Two adjoining rooms, in cash, with a little extra to sweeten the deal."

The young man leaned forward, and Cassie placed her arm over the money. "Do we have a deal?"

Crawford rolled his eyes and nodded.

"Great," Cassie said. "And we'd like rooms on the back of the motel."

"Rooms on the front are renovated."

"We don't mind."

"Fine. Rooms 103 and 104," he said, passing key cards through a machine. "Check out is at eleven o'clock, and we don't have a continental breakfast."

"Thanks." Cassie took the cards and headed for the door.

"Wait. I need to grab you some towels."

Cassie stopped short. "Sorry?"

"We don't use the back rooms much. Everything's clean back there, but there are no towels. Rats get them. Wait here."

He disappeared into the back office. Surely he wasn't serious?

A squeaky hinged cupboard opened, and Crawford came back, bearing four surprisingly white towels.

"There are rats in the back rooms?"

"Used to be, but the health inspector made us put out some bait boxes. Should be good now." Cassie ignored the shudder that ran down her spine and took the towels from his hands.

It took everything within her not to throw the towels back at him and run from the office. She swallowed hard and turned for the door. One thing was for sure, the next time she saw Gerald, they were going to have a little chat about these meet spots.

Cassie let out a slow breath, refusing to think about what Crawford had just told her. Instead, she waved Ryan to drive around back and meet her there. She stood outside her motel room and waited for Duke and Ryan to get out of the Jeep. Now that the prospect of sleep was at hand, it was all she could think of.

"Everything alright?" Ryan asked.

"Of course. Two adjoining rooms. No questions," she said, plopping his room key into his hand. Without another word, she went into her room focused solely on getting some shut-eye.

Ryan stuck his foot in the door, and she stared at him, puzzled when he followed her in. "Duke's going to stay with you, okay?" he said.

"Fine." She sighed, collapsing with exhaustion onto the bed. The back of her mind registered that he unlocked the door adjoining their two rooms and grabbed a couple of the towels.

"You need anything, anything at all, you come on through, don't worry about knocking."

"Okay," she mumbled.

"You should call the Marshals and let them know where we are."

Cassie's eyes drifted shut.

"Cassie…"

"I will," she mumbled. "I just need to close my eyes. Just for a minute," Cassie said, slipping into slumber. She barely registered his touch gently shaking her shoulder. He was saying something, but she was too tired. The next thing she heard was the hotel room door softly shutting.

Rolling over, Cassie let one eye pop open. *What time was it?*

The blackout drapes kept the room dark. Pushing the pillows out of the way, she glanced at the clock. It was 9:00 a.m.

Every muscle in Cassie's back throbbed, and her knee ached. She looked over at Duke, who lay on the edge of her bed.

"Time to get up, buddy," she said and ruffled the fur behind his ears.

He whined and shuffled away from her.

Cassie smiled. "I hear you, Duke. Me too."

She stretched out her back and ran her tongue

over her fuzzy teeth. As much as she longed to go back to sleep, she knew a shower was what she needed. She grabbed a towel from the top of the dresser and opened it up only to discover a rusty brown stain down its inside. *You've got to be kidding me.* Disgusted, Cassie dropped the towel onto the floor and inspected the other, only to find it was just as bad.

Grumbling under her breath, Cassie stuffed her feet into her boots and let the door slam behind her. The bright morning sun burned her eyes, sharpening her mood. Temper flaring, she trudged over the slushy walk to the office.

The bell jangled over the door as Cassie marched across the green shag carpet to the counter.

"Hello," Cassie called. "Crawford?" She began ringing the bell on the edge of the counter. "Hello?"

No one emerged from the back. The Ludlow certainly wasn't The Ritz, but the very least they could do was provide a clean towel to take a shower with. Was that too much to ask? Cassie rang the bell for the second time, but the door to the office remained firmly shut. This was completely unacceptable. All she needed was a couple of towels, and she knew where they were.

Cassie stepped behind the counter, her pulse quickening. *It's just towels*, she admonished herself. *It's not like I'm stealing them.* Taking a deep breath, she walked boldly into the back office.

An old utility sink stood at her right hip, with the water left running full blast into it. Cassie snapped the tap off and almost knocked the measuring cup of cleaner from its ledge. She looked around the sad space. The wall across from her held a broken rolltop desk laden with papers, a plate with a half-eaten sandwich and coffee that was still steaming.

Definitely not The Ritz, she thought. On the other side of the utility sink was a short wall of cupboards. She opened the first door to discover a mop, bucket and toilet supplies. Quickly closing it, she opened the second cupboard, and Crawford fell heavily on top of her, knocking her to the concrete floor.

Limp limbs tangled with hers as she pushed at the body, desperate to get it off of her. When it finally rolled to the side, Cassie scrambled backward, jamming her back painfully into the desk.

The lifeless desk clerk lay sprawled across the dirty floor, his neck twisted at an impossible angle.

Her stomach roiled, and she wildly swiped at her arms and legs, desperate to erase the sensations of being entangled with the clammy body. Crawford's frozen eyes bore into hers, spiraling a warning through her.

"Ryan," she murmured.

Rushing for the phone on the desk, Cassie's fingers quickly dialed Ryan's room.

"Hello?" Ryan's voice sounded groggy.

"The desk clerk, he's dead." For a moment, there was no answer.

"What?"

"The desk clerk is dead."

"The Wolf?"

"I don't know. Maybe," Cassie said, trying to pull herself together. Was Crawford's death a result of something in his own life? Or had The Wolf eliminated him because he was in the wrong place at the wrong time? With the facts she had, there was no way to know for sure.

"Where are you?"

Ryan's words snapped her back to the present. "The office."

She could hear him moving around the motel room. "Get out of there," he said, sounding wide-awake now. "I'm on my way to you."

Cassie hung up the phone as the door frame whined behind her, making the hairs on the back of her neck rise.

"I've waited a long time for this," came a deep whisper.

Cassie scanned the desk, looking for something, anything that she could use as a weapon. "Don't take it personally, but I was hoping never to meet you," she said without turning around. Keeping her movements small, Cassie deliberately placed her hand next to a stack of bills on the desk. She took a breath and swiveled her chair to face The Wolf.

He stood unassuming, not even three feet away from her. His hawklike face held cold, intelligent eyes that dissected and devoured. Cassie shivered.

"I've played this moment around in my mind for a long time. Funny, I always imagined you screaming in it," The Wolf said.

"I could if you'd like."

"No, I prefer this," he said, moving closer. His arm snaked out, and Cassie flinched when he grasped a lock of her hair. "You look so different." His head tilted. "I like the red." He drew her jaw upward, forcing her to meet his gaze. A faint smile turned the corners of his lips, and he began reciting:

"Cream white roses herald the passage,
Swan wings to carry you away.
On bended knee, I'll gild the message,
Your soul was never meant to stay."

His eyes began probing hers, and Cassie snapped her lids shut. But closing her eyes couldn't block the feeling. His thumb and forefinger ran down either side of her neck until they stopped midway.

"Your pulse is racing." The Wolf gently shook her, forcing her to look at him. "Whether you say it or not, I know you fear me."

Cassie's eyes narrowed, her chin rising.

He smirked. "So much moxie. Not many have that these days." His hands dropped to his sides. "You're special, Cassie. I could tell from the sketches and paintings you did of me. It's like you froze that moment just before the congressman died. I look at that painting almost every day."

"Look at it? You have it?" she whispered.

"I have all of them, the sketches and the paintings. They're hanging on my walls at home. I couldn't let the police keep the gifts you'd meant for me. Your brilliance, the way your brushstrokes speak of your love for me, it was all wasted on them." He leaned down and whispered against Cassie's ear, "Now, it's my turn to honor you as you did me. I want to set you free."

Cassie lunged upward with a letter opener. Catching The Wolf off guard, she stabbed him in the shoulder, making him stumble backward. She bolted for the door, falling hard against the door frame when his muscular body crashed into hers. His fingers twined through her hair and pulled her head back.

"You'll pay for that."

Cassie saw the measuring cup of bleach. Her hand darted out, and before he could stop her, she tossed the cleaner blindly over her shoulder. He grunted, and his grip loosened. She sprinted out of the office into the middle of the abandoned parking lot.

A semitruck on the highway let out its air brakes. Where was Ryan?

The door chimes angrily clanked, turning her attention back to the office door. The Wolf emerged and squinted at her through puffy red eyes. His face dripped with water from where he'd probably doused himself under the tap. He took a cautious step toward her. Cassie's chest knotted with terror. She had no weapon, no money, nowhere to go.

Her red Jeep flew around the corner of the motel and spun sideways between her and The Wolf. Ryan slammed the Jeep into Park and leaped out of the vehicle while The Wolf retreated into the woods.

Ryan ran toward her. "Are you okay?" he asked. His eyes frantically searching her body for wounds.

"I will be."

"Get in the Jeep and stay low. Any sign of trouble, and I want you to get out of here. Don't wait for me," he said before running toward the woods with his gun drawn.

"Ryan, don't do this."

"Just get in the Jeep," he yelled, disappearing into the densely packed trees.

For once, Cassie did as she was told, but her mind quickly became fixed on its own plan. She moved her vehicle to the edge of the lot, a place that provided a quick getaway should it become necessary. Then, reaching into the back seat, Cassie pushed Duke out of the way and retrieved the duffel. Finding her gun and Linux phone, she dialed the number that had long since been committed to memory.

The phone rang plaintively in her ear while she sank low in her seat. First, she was requesting backup to this location and then she was going after Ryan, whether he liked it or not.

Gunshots punctuated the quiet morning. "Pick up. Come on, pick up," Cassie said, looking for movement in the trees, her heart pounding.

"Gerald Hawkins, Tax Specialists Office," a perky female voice said.

"This is client 9-8 Lima Tango 6-1-7 Alpha."

"What is your access code?"

"White Stone."

"Please hold while I connect you with your control marshal."

"Hello, Cassandra, this is Tess."

Cassie sat up. "Where's Gerald?"

"He's not able to assist right now, but I am. What's happening, Cassandra?"

Alarm pounded through Cassie's body. This didn't feel right; something was wrong. "I don't know you," she said.

"Cassandra, I am with the US Marshals office. You can trust me."

"I only speak with Gerald."

The phone line went quiet.

"Cassandra, Gerald is dead."

"Dead?" she heard herself whisper.

"What is your current location?"

"How did he die?"

"That's not relevant. I'm here to assist you. What is your current location?"

"It *is* relevant. How did he die?"

"Cassandra…"

"If you want my trust, then you're going to tell me. How did he die?"

There was a long pause on the phone.

"He was shot."

"By who?"

"We don't know."

"When?"

"Last week."

Cassie leaned forward, her head resting on the cold steering wheel.

Gerald, her lifeline, the man who had prayed with her in her darkest days and told the worst punny jokes, was dead. Her brain struggled around the word, unable to come to terms with it. This had to be some sort of mistake.

"I don't think you heard me right. I need to speak to Gerald. Gerald Hawkins," Cassie insisted, her voice cracking.

"Cassandra, I'm really sorry. I know that the two of you were close."

Her chest felt hollow as thick tears caked on her eyelashes. This couldn't be happening. Not Gerald. And especially not shot. He was too good of a marshal, too alert. Cassie's thoughts began to spin. Had he been killed because of her? Had The Wolf gotten to him? Cassie couldn't shake the idea, her soul feeling heavy with the weight of it.

The phone lay on her lap, with Tess barking for attention.

Her stomach turned when another thought crossed her mind. If The Wolf killed Gerald, how did he know that Gerald was her control marshal? And for that matter, how had he found her here at the Ludlow Motel or even Bakerton? Cassie pressed the heels of her palms to her eyes. She needed to think. Something wasn't right about all of this, and the one common denominator among all her questions was the US Marshals' office.

Taking a deep breath, she hung up the phone. She couldn't trust the Marshals right now. Cassie stared absently at the woods when Ryan emerged from the tree line, his eyes bright from the chase. He was not going to like what she had just done.

"Let's go," he said, hopping into the passenger seat beside her.

"What happened?" Cassie asked and shifted the Jeep into gear.

"The bush got pretty thick back there… I lost him."

"I'm sorry, Ryan," Cassie said, her voice hollow.

"What're you sorry for? I'm the one that lost him."

"But I'm the one that brought you here." Cassie blinked back tears. Gerald was dead, The Wolf was on her heels and the Marshals were compromised. Could this get any worse? "The motel was supposed to be safe."

"Cassie, this isn't on you," Ryan said softly.

"Yes, it is," she said. "I called in like I'm supposed to, but I…but Gerald…" She gritted her teeth, the words making her stomach feel sour. She didn't want to say them, but she had to. "…my control marshal, he was murdered last week."

"Why weren't you notified?"

"All I know is that he's dead, and Crawford is dead and Logan..."

His hand gripped her shoulder. "This is not on you. You didn't pull the trigger."

"I may as well have." She looked over at him. "Now I've got you mixed up in all of this."

"Cassie..."

"I don't want to hear it. I'll take you as far as Portland, and then I'm dropping you off."

"And then what?"

Cassie's grip tightened on the steering wheel. "I'll figure something out."

"Really? That's how you're going to play this. I'm an FBI agent."

"Used to be an FBI agent. You *used* to be an FBI agent." She could feel his eyes burn holes into the side of her head. "You have a life and a job in Bakerton," she continued, "you can't go on the run with me."

"But I can see you set up somewhere safe," Ryan said.

"Why would you want to?"

"Are you serious right now?" he said, his voice harsh with irritation.

She didn't care if she hurt his feelings. She wasn't willing to give an inch, not today. "I'm dropping you off in Portland."

"You might be my ex-girlfriend, Cassie, but

that doesn't mean I want to see you hurt or dead." He twisted in his seat, leveling those impossibly blue eyes on her. "There was a time when you meant a lot to me. Let me do my job and protect you."

His words hit her chest as hard as a hammer. *There was a time.* Was—past tense. She gripped the steering wheel tighter, trying hard to concentrate on the road.

"Don't say stuff like that," Cassie said, practically choking on the words.

"But it's true."

Cassie shook her head. This was all too much. On every front, she was being battered and torn. Her eyes burned from fighting back the tears. "No." Her voice cracked. "You're reminding me of what was between us to get me to do what you want. That's not fair."

"Is that what you think I'm doing?" His eyes narrowed.

Cassie said nothing. She couldn't say anything, so she let the silence speak for her.

"Please," he said, leaning toward her, "let me help you get somewhere safe. It's a week until Christmas, and the thought of you out there, alone…" His sentence dangled. "I've got contacts and old friends that you could use right about now."

If she were honest, part of her wanted to say

no, to stop the Jeep, to let him walk the rest of the way to Portland. Make him feel like he'd meant nothing to her for a change, make him pay for those tortured nights she'd cried herself to sleep. But where would that get her? Her indignation and hurt warred with practicality. She wasn't helpless, her pride argued. She could manage just fine on her own... *Pride goeth before destruction, and an haughty spirit before a fall. Proverbs 16:18.* Cassie let out an annoyed sigh.

"For a day or two at most, and then we go our separate ways," Cassie finally spit out. "If you can agree to that, then you've got a deal."

"I can agree with that." Ryan paused cautiously. "Do you think we could stop in Dalton?"

"Why?" Cassie asked.

"I need you to meet my friend, Patrick."

FIVE

While Ryan was a good man, he was also a very stubborn one, especially—as it turned out—where Cassie's safety was concerned. He had almost come unglued when she insisted on stopping at the ranch store in Dalton to get him some new clothes. But she was driving, and he had finally agreed that walking around in a bloodied cop uniform was due to attract attention. The pit stop only took fifteen minutes, and the way Cassie saw it, they had at least an hour before The Wolf could track them again. Bleach in the eyes was not something to be ignored.

Ryan may have conceded the stop for clothing, but he would not give up on the idea that The Wolf had placed a tracking device on her Jeep. And nothing made stubbornness more infuriating than when the other person had a good chance of being right. He was determined that they change vehicles. She wasn't sure she agreed with his assessment on the tracker, but she had to admit swapping out her Jeep was smart. Red was a rather eye-catching color.

"Exactly where are we going, Ryan?" Cassie asked as she drove the Jeep down Dry Hollow Road on the outskirts of Dalton City. Under different circumstances, the road would have made for a lovely drive as they meandered over rolling hills, past farmhouses decked out in Christmas decor and by snow-covered orchards that flanked the road on both sides.

"I'll know it when I see it. Look, you need to trust me on this. I know you think what's happened back at the Ludlow is the Marshals' fault, but I've worked with them before. They wouldn't leak your location," he said earnestly. "You were so exhausted you didn't even phone them until after The Wolf ambushed us at the motel."

Cassie couldn't disagree with Ryan's logic, but it also didn't explain everything. Like how did The Wolf find her in Bakerton? Until that question was answered, she couldn't bring herself to trust the Marshals again. Trying to puzzle it out, she said, "The Ludlow was a registered location that I'd go to if I was in trouble. Anyone with access to my file would know that."

"A marshal would never give up that information. The GPS tracker is the best explanation for The Wolf dogging us."

While his words about the Marshals fit her own experience with them, her gut warned her they were compromised.

"Let's not spend the whole drive arguing," she said, taking a sip of her coffee. "Where is this place?"

"It should be coming up soon." Ryan's casual gaze caught the side-view mirror, and his posture stiffened. "You keep your Jeep well serviced, right?" he asked, manually cranking open the passenger window to adjust the side mirror, sending cold wind whistling through the Jeep.

"Of course." The tone in Ryan's voice nailed a spike of fear through Cassie's heart. She checked the rearview. A gray SUV was approaching fast. With the roads as snowy as they were, no responsible motorist would be driving like that. Cassie pressed her foot harder on the accelerator. "You think it's The Wolf?"

"Him or one of his teams," Ryan said, pulling his gun from its holster, his eyes trained on the mirror. "Either way, I don't think they're friendlies back there."

"How many are in the vehicle?" Cassie asked, rounding a corner so fast the Jeep leaned precariously close to going onto two wheels.

Ryan grabbed the plastic Jeep safety handle located above the glove box. "I don't have a good visual," he said, twisting in his seat to watch the vehicle come around the corner behind them. "But it looks like one driver and one passenger. If I had to guess, I'd say both males."

The road straightened out, and Cassie let the engine rev as she punched the gas. A gun fired from the SUV, and a bullet struck her tailgate, making Duke howl from the back seat. Cassie held the Jeep to the road, but the rear of her vehicle fishtailed from the hit, tossing up sprays of snow while they swayed from side to side.

"Duck," Ryan yelled when another volley of bullets erupted from behind them. Cassie scrunched low over the steering wheel and swung the vehicle around a sloping turn.

"How's Duke?"

Ryan looked into the back seat, giving the dog a hand command to stay low. "He's fine," he said, staring out the rear window. "Come on, Cassie, you're going to have to drive faster than this. They're gaining on us."

"Not helping," Cassie said, looking in her side mirror and silently praying. Winter driving was not her favorite at the best of times, and in this situation, it only served to magnify her anxiety. Within moments, the SUV could overtake them, and what would she do then?

"Frost heave."

"What?" Cassie said, drawing her attention back to the road and the large heave that lay in their path. There was no time to brake; they were going way too fast. The nose of the Jeep climbed high into the air, sending a weightless feeling through Cassie's stomach. Then as quickly as it rose, the Jeep tilted downward. For a second, Cassie thought the vehicle was going to roll end over end, then the front tires hit the pavement with a hard bounce followed by the rear wheels.

"Nice," Ryan said, giving Cassie an approving nod.

"Where are we going?" she asked.

Ryan analyzed their surroundings. "You're getting close to a T-intersection. It's just on the other side of this rise. When you get there, you're going to make a hard left and stay on Dry Hollow Road."

"A hard left?" Cassie looked down at her speedometer. "At this speed?"

He met her eyes with calm confidence. "Once you reach the top of this hill, slow it down to second gear speeds, then lots of gas. The Jeep is going to start sliding, and you'll naturally oversteer to compensate. That should send the rear of the Jeep into big pendulum swings."

Cassie's heart lodged in her throat as she neared the crest in the road.

"Try to time the drifts of your swing to help you around the bend at the bottom. You've got this. I know you do."

Reaching the top, she stared ominously down at the intersection.

"Keep your foot smooth on the gas pedal," Ryan said calmly, "and your eyes tracking the road."

On its descent, the Jeep jostled over compact snow that had washboarded the road, making everything vibrate. It slid sideways, and Cassie braked rhythmically, timing the pendulum-like swings to help her around the tight corner. As they came out of the turn, Ryan whooped with triumph, but Cassie barely heard him. She just hammered the gas pedal, sending them roaring up the next hill.

"They're still behind us," Ryan said, looking out the side mirror, "and coming up fast."

Cassie raced the Jeep as fast as she dared but knew her old vehicle was no match for the SUV. She needed to level the playing field, but she had never driven off the main streets of Dalton before and had no idea where the rutted service roads between orchards led. Any one of them could lead to freedom or bury them chassis-deep in snow. She glanced in her rearview mirror. The SUV was edging dangerously close to her bumper. If it came alongside or rammed the Jeep from behind, they would be done for.

Cassie spared Ryan a glance. "You know any of these side roads?"

"No." He grimaced, then nodded. "But you're right. They're our best shot at getting out of this. If you think you're going to get stuck in the snow, try to swing the passenger side outward, and I'll give you cover fire while you run for it."

"They'll kill you." Her heart clenched in her chest.

"No arguing, Cassie," Ryan said, readying his gun. "Swing the passenger side out, and you run. You don't stop running until you're safe. You got it?"

He met her eyes, and the fire she saw within them let her know there was no use in fighting.

"Ryan—"

"You run, Cassie."

She let out a slow breath. "Let's hope it doesn't come to that. Up here on the right, six hundred yards."

Ryan gripped the safety handle in front of him, bracing himself for the hard corner they were about to take. The Jeep slid on ice through the turn, kicking up clouds of snow while they spun. Cassie pumped the brake, then accelerated when she gained control, making the engine growl plaintively.

"They missed the turn," Ryan called over his shoulder. "Make this baby hustle, Cassie."

Up the hill, she raced past sheds and around sharp turns, following the well-worn ruts and praying that the track she was on didn't turn out to be a dead end. So far, she had been fortunate the snow was only a few inches deep, and the dirt road beneath the tires was providing excellent traction. Still, it wouldn't take long for the SUV to catch up.

"And they're back," Ryan said, his eyes glued to the side mirror. A hail of bullets erupted from behind them, shattering the back window.

"Hold on." Cassie swung the vehicle to the left through a wide path in the orchard.

"What're you doing?"

"They won't follow us through here," Cassie called while she tore through the deep snow. "They'll get stuck." It didn't take long for the heavy white powder to begin caking around her front tires and pushing up over the front bumper onto the hood. Despite the mire, her

Jeep trudged on. The engine worked hard but continued to blaze a path through the orchard.

"They're still behind us," Ryan said.

Cassie glowered at the rearview. Sure enough, the SUV chased after them. Undeterred by her efforts, it followed in their tracks, refusing to give up and gaining on them.

Frustrated, she pulled her gaze away and watched the path ahead. The trees began narrowing their route, causing branches to scrape down the sides of her vehicle. If it got much tighter, they would have to stop and make a run for it.

The SUV rammed into the back of their vehicle, lurching Cassie forward against her seat belt. Duke let out a small whimper but lay secure on the floor. Cassie accelerated, pushing the engine as the SUV backed off and gathered momentum to hit them again.

"Turn down there," Ryan said, pointing down an aisle of trees up ahead.

With a quick twist of the wheel, Cassie swung the Jeep, causing a wave of snow, and sped down the hill. The Jeep shimmied and bucked at the quick change in direction, but thankfully pressed on. Relief flooded through her until she looked up ahead. At the end of the row stood a fence with a small gap that led into a pasture. It was going to make for a tight fit, but there was a chance they could make it. She cast a brief glance at Ryan.

"You've got this," he said.

There was no room for error. Cassie pointed the Jeep at the hole in the fence and did not back down. She floored the gas pedal, her eyes riveted to the fence. They barreled through the opening, the side mirrors ripping off the Jeep as they went. Cassie looked through the rearview.

The SUV was too wide to pass through the fence. At a high rate of speed, it hit the large post on the passenger side, shearing off the fence rails and launching the vehicle onto its side. The SUV slid, kicking up dirt and snow until it teetered, falling onto its roof. Cassie slowed the Jeep until she saw the two men from the SUV begin to pull themselves out of the vehicle.

"Don't stop!" Ryan yelled, and Cassie stepped on the gas. Bullets peppered the ground behind them, but at this distance, they were out of range. She spied an open cattle gate and went through it onto an old country back road.

Relieved that they had survived, Cassie reached over and squeezed Ryan's hand. "I didn't think we were going to make it."

He shook his head in disbelief. "Neither did I."

"Where to now?"

"We need to ditch this vehicle and fast. Let me call my buddy and have him meet us."

Not even a half hour later, Cassie stared at her Jeep in disbelief. It sat in the middle of a Quonset hut on Ryan's friend's property while two burly men harvested it for parts. If she weren't watching it, she wouldn't have believed how fast they were stripping her vehicle down to the shiny metal. Unable to stomach the sight, Cassie grabbed the black duffel bag and walked out of the hut.

"We didn't have a choice," Ryan said, following her out.

A lump rose in her throat. He didn't understand what that vehicle meant to her. After assuming the identity of Cassie Whitfield, her first purchase had been that bright red Jeep. While it was *only a vehicle*, it had physically moved her from the darkest point in her life to a town that had given her a colorful new beginning, filled with people she loved. Cassie knew she was acting overly sentimental, but part of her felt she owed the Jeep a better end than this.

"It's been with me through a lot," she said and changed the subject. "We've been here too long. Where's this truck your friend promised?"

Ryan gently turned her to face him. With no choice but to stare up into the light blue pools of his eyes, Cassie's breath caught in her chest. He was a very good-looking man, and no matter how hard she tried to ignore that detail, her heart refused to let her forget it.

"I know that Jeep meant something to you, but Patrick didn't feel safe driving it with how quickly The Wolf's men found us after leaving the Ludlow. There simply wasn't enough time to thoroughly check it for tracking devices," Ryan said. "The money he makes from selling off the parts will cover the cost of the truck. It's a good deal, Cassie."

She looked down, unable to bear the sympathy within his eyes. "I understand," she said.

"Duke's in the truck." Ryan nodded toward their new vehicle that sat a short distance away. "But if you need some time, the boys are about to haul away what's left of your Jeep. You can take a moment if you need to."

With a shrug of her shoulder, she shook off his touch. "Better get going," she said and held out her hand for the new set of keys.

"Cassie—"

"It's fine, Ryan. Honestly, it's fine," she said and began walking toward the truck. Her life was exploding, and no matter what she seemed to do, the losses just kept piling up.

Cassie sidestepped a muddy puddle and unlocked the rear passenger side door. Duke lifted his sleepy head and looked at her, puzzled. She placed the black duffel onto the floor of the truck when Duke stretched up and licked her nose. Startled by his tenderness, Cassie blinked back tears and burrowed her face into his fur. He was simply the best dog ever.

The reality of her situation hit like a tidal wave. Life in Bakerton was over. She was not ever going to see any of her friends again. Tears threatened to spill down her cheeks. "Can you tell Sarah that if she wants it, I'll give her my restaurant. I can sign papers once we get somewhere safe." Cassie swiped at the dampness on her cheeks. "Tell her I'm sorry that I couldn't say goodbye."

Ryan moved closer. Concern etched on his brow. "Are you okay?"

"Yeah," she said, stepping back from him too quickly. "I think I do need that moment."

His lips twisted thoughtfully. "Why don't you take Duke for a walk?" he said.

Hearing the word *walk* made Duke's ears perk up, and before Cassie could respond, he bounced out of the truck, wriggling like an overgrown puppy.

"Well, who could say no to that?" Cassie smiled wanly.

As Ryan bent down to clip the leash to his collar, Duke jumped up playfully and knocked Ryan onto his backside in the mud. Ryan sat stunned, his hands disappearing under the thick muck of the puddle. Duke didn't miss a beat. He bounded and splashed, pelting Ryan's face with dirty water.

"Duke," Ryan groaned, "stop it, buddy." But the dog had been cooped up for most of the day and was eager to play. His front paws came up onto Ryan's shoulders, and he began licking the splatters from his master's face. Being no small dog, he came close to bowling Ryan over into the mud again. Laughing, Ryan pushed the dog off and looked up at Cassie with sparkling eyes. "I could use a hand," he said, reaching his muddied fingers toward her.

She took an amused step back. "Yeah, no. I don't think so," she said. Duke buried his nose in the mud, snorted and then rolled gleefully, causing a spray of water that Cassie narrowly avoided.

Ryan grabbed ahold of a long stick and waved it in the air. "Hey, buddy," he said, gaining Duke's attention. The dog, spying what Ryan held, began vibrating with excitement. "Go fetch." And with that, Ryan threw the stick as far as he could down the road. Duke took off like a shot after it, sending a hail of mud across Ryan's face. "Yuck." He grimaced, wiping his cheek with the arm of his hoodie.

Covering her lips, Cassie couldn't help but laugh. "Enjoying your shower?"

"Immensely," he said, lifting his hand toward her again. "So, are you going to help a guy out or what?"

Ominously, Cassie stared at the offering and then at him, not trusting the grin he was trying to suppress.

"I'll behave. I promise," he said, innocently. "Please?"

With a skeptical sigh, Cassie stepped forward and reached down, helping Ryan up to his full height. Suddenly, her feet slipped toward him in the mud, and they crashed together, his arms locking around her for stability. The laughter between them evaporated. She looked up into his penetrating eyes, eyes that no longer sheltered suspicion. Cassie's heart raced, her gaze dropping to his lips as he drew her closer. Her head tilted slightly when something sharp poked the back of her calf.

Duke nudged her again with his stick, eager for her to throw it.

Cassie shook her head and stepped out of Ryan's hold. What was she doing? This couldn't happen, not now, not when she was running for her life. Duke dropped the stick at her feet, and she reached down to pat his soft furry head. Thank the Lord for Duke. A few more seconds and she would have kissed Ryan, and that would havc complicated everything. Shc dared to look up and found Ryan's eyes glued to hers with questions that she didn't want to answer.

Hastily, Cassie grabbed the wet leash from Ryan's hand. "Come on, Duke," she said, her hands slightly trembling as she clipped the leash onto the dog's collar. Before she could say or do anything more that she would regret, Cassie strode off down the dirt road without a backward glance.

When she returned twenty minutes later, Ryan was sitting on the end of the tailgate in fresh clothes, and she sheepishly hopped up beside him. On her walk, she had rehearsed all the reasons why getting involved with him again was a mistake. But now, sitting beside him, all those words vanished. The sunset had stolen the last of the day's warmth, and she rubbed her hands together, blowing on them, trying to think of what to say.

"Good walk?" Ryan asked, breaking the strained silence.

"Yeah. Look, about earlier..."

"Cassie, don't," he said.

"Don't what?"

"I'm pretty sure I know what you're going to say. Let's just let it be what it was—a leftover spark from another time."

Disappointment washed over her, and Cassie found herself surprised by it. She should be grateful that she didn't have to have an awkward conversation, and yet she wasn't. Nothing made sense.

Ryan slid off the back of the truck and stood facing her. "Why don't I get this guy cleaned up while you change out of those muddy clothes," he said.

She looked down at her dirty coat and jeans before casually nodding in agreement. When Cassie returned, Duke sat on the tailgate, his eyes sparkling while Ryan tucked the dog's food dishes into the truck box.

Why did she suddenly feel like an eighth-grader whose friend had exposed her first crush to the class? This was silly. "We should get going," Cassie said, suddenly eager to put as much distance as she could between herself and this place. Cassie took Duke's leash and tapped her thigh. Duke hopped down obediently, and Cassie was careful to keep the leash tight to avoid another mud puddle mishap. While she tucked Duke into the truck's back seat, she felt Ryan come up behind her. Her stomach fluttered with nerves. "I was thinking we could head to Los Angeles," Cassie said, not turning around. "It's a big city. A good place for me to disappear."

Ryan said nothing. She closed the rear door, her heart beating quickly.

"While you were gone on your walk, I phoned my former partner at the FBI."

Cassie whipped around to face him. "You what?"

"Just hear me out," Ryan said, holding up his hands in mock surrender.

The last thing she wanted to do was listen. What was Ryan thinking? He had no business making a plan and getting other people involved without talking to her first. She didn't need another person to get hurt because of her.

"Kate is a solid agent," Ryan stated.

"I'm sure she is."

"She has excellent connections with the US Marshals Service."

"I'm not going back into WITSEC," Cassie said, crossing her arms over her chest. "And you'd know that if you'd bothered to ask me."

"Cassie," Ryan pleaded, "be logical."

Be logical. Her eyes narrowed into burning slits. "I'm not going back, and that's not negotiable."

"Come on, at least meet with her."

"I don't want any more people involved in

this, Ryan. Two people are dead, and one is badly injured because of me."

"That's not your fault," he said, trying to sound calm. The rigid line of his jaw told her otherwise. "The Wolf isn't some neighborhood thug. You, of all people, shouldn't need reminding of that. You need Kate, and you need the Marshals."

"*I* decide what *I* need. *Me*," Cassie said, pointing at herself. "You don't get to make those choices without talking to me first."

"WITSEC is your best option."

She didn't have time for this argument. Cassie reached into the truck, yanked out her duffel bag and slung it over her shoulder. She never should have taken him along.

"What are you doing?"

She raised her chin. "We're not that far from town. Keep the truck, Ryan. It's the least I can do for all the problems I've caused you, but this isn't going to work."

"What are you talking about?" he said, stepping in front of her.

"You've decided my future without consulting me," Cassie responded incredulously. "That's not how partnerships work. That's not how *we* work."

He stared at her, not moving, his lack of a retort speaking a million words. He had overstepped, and watching that realization play across his face took some of the wind out of her temper.

"I'm sorry," Cassie said, her voice softer. "I am, but this is my future, and I get to choose it." She rose on her tiptoes and lightly kissed his temple, the smell of him flooding her senses. "I will be okay," she whispered, unable to stop her fingers from lightly caressing the stubble on his jaw. Surprised by the feelings that swelled within her, Cassie turned from him abruptly and began following the dirt road toward town. This was for the best.

The truck door slammed, and before she knew it, the vehicle's tires were creaking along the road slowly beside her. Ryan rolled down the window, and Cassie's spine bristled, her temper flaring back to life. Couldn't he respect her choices just once?

"Get in the truck."

"No."

Ryan gave a loud disgruntled sigh. "I shouldn't have called Kate without talking to you first."

"You're right about that."

"I'm sorry," he said earnestly, but Cassie continued to put one foot in front of the other, refusing to truly hear his words. He honked the horn, making her jump.

Slowly, Cassie turned her head toward him, her gaze lethal. "Leave me alone," she said and resumed walking.

"And then how would I know you were safe? Would you really leave me to wonder for the rest of my life if you're alive or dead in a ditch somewhere? Don't go. Not like this."

His tone pulled at the strings of her heart. Her quick steps faltered until she stood still. She stared up into the darkening sky. *God, why did You make men so impossible?* Cassie sighed.

"I messed up."

Gritting her teeth, she could feel her resolve begin to lessen. Her gaze met his, and it was like being caught in the ocean's undertow. She was consumed with emotion, feeling the deep concern that sat on his face plain as day. Cassie turned away and glowered at the ground.

The truck door opened, and she could feel his presence come up behind her.

"Please," he said tenderly. "I would really like it if you got in the truck."

Her shoulders sagged. She couldn't afford to lose her voice in this journey. "We have to make decisions together."

"Always."

Cassie closed her eyes, her thoughts spinning. She didn't have an exact plan. She didn't know where she should go or what to do when she got there. Was being with Ryan so bad? At least with him she wasn't alone, and she had someone to bounce ideas off of. Cassie took a deep breath and gave Ryan a wide berth when she walked back to the truck. She slid into the passenger seat, wondering all the while if she was making a mistake.

Together, they drove off down the bumpy road, twilight moving into darkness. After a while, Cassie broke the silence. "I can't handle another death on my conscience."

"I hear you, and I can understand that," he said, keeping his eyes on the road, "but The Wolf is going to come after us again, and he's better prepared than we are. I know I approached this wrong, but Kate is one of the FBI's best. Even if you're firm on leaving WITSEC, we could use an ally like her on our side."

Cassie didn't like it, but she couldn't deny the truth to his statement. The Wolf excelled at the hunt, and they had very limited resources at their disposal.

"I'm sorry about earlier," Ryan said, sensing her wavering, "but please, don't let my mistake cost you our best asset."

Cassie gazed out the passenger window, her wounded pride throbbing. She hated to admit it but having someone with active connections to FBI resources would be a big help. It was hard not to choke on the words, but she spoke them all the same. “Does Kate live far from here?”

“Not too far, about an hour or two. You won’t regret this.” Ryan smiled.

“I sure hope I don’t,” Cassie said, turning on the radio.

SIX

Icy snow pelted hard against the basement windows, making Cassie thankful they were off the road. It had taken closer to three hours to reach Kate's place on the outskirts of Troutdale, but it had felt like forever. The darkness had hidden most of the beauty of the meandering Historic Columbia River Highway, but Ryan assured her that come daylight, she would be impressed by the wooded charm of her surroundings.

Stroking Duke with her foot, Cassie sat patiently on the basement couch and waited for Ryan to finish his turn. The last thing she wanted to do was play darts, but Ryan had pushed her into a quick game of 301. It was obvious that he was trying to distract her from her thoughts until Kate was home, and his stories of catching Chinook salmon on the Sandy River outback were not doing the trick. Ryan threw his last dart, and it bounced off the board. He looked sheepishly over at Cassie. "Even when your heart isn't in it, you still beat me," he said, taking a seat.

A smile spread across her face as she stepped over Duke to take her place. "Winters are cold in North Dakota, and my brothers weren't inclined to play tea party for long." She readied the dart in her right hand, let her stance fall into place and threw her three darts, hitting a triple, a single and a double. Cassie retrieved her darts and sat back on the plaid couch.

Ryan turned to her with a warm smile. "So, you do have a family?"

"I do." Her heart swelled. "Two older brothers, Jacob and Matthew." It felt like an eternity had passed since she had last hugged them or been prey to one of their stunts. "You know, I can't even remember the last time I've said their names out loud." Her eyes closed, savoring the freedom.

"What are they like?"

Cassie relaxed against the couch and pulled her knees up to her chest. "Both fiercely loyal," she laughed. "They'd tease and play harmless pranks, but they wouldn't let anyone else do the same to me." She closed her eyes and imagined their faces. "They were good about including me. Whether it was fishing or darts, football or board games, I was welcome to join so long as I could keep up. My grandparents always..." Ryan tilted his head, and she felt his unspoken question. "That part of what I told you is true," she said, catching his gaze. "My parents died when I was two in a boating accident. But instead of foster care, my grandparents raised my brothers and me."

"I'm sorry about your parents."

"Me too," she said, taking a deep breath. "I don't really remember them, but my brothers and grandparents retell their stories so often, I feel like they are my own memories."

"Sounds like you were a close family."

"My parents' death bound us together. That was the hardest part of joining WITSEC—losing my family. We were always together."

"Is that why you're so good with a gun? Your brothers?" Ryan asked.

"No, that was Gerald," Cassie said tenderly. "The FBI had me stationed at this safe house in the middle of nowhere, with nothing to do, while we waited for WITSEC to process my paperwork. One evening, Gerald came by doing his regular check-in. He wanted to play chess, but for the life of me, I couldn't stomach another game." Her fingers absently toyed with the handle on her mug of tea. "Gerald had this stare, and it would only last for a couple of seconds, but it was like he could see right through to your soul. He gave me one of those and then said, 'Right then, come with me,' and walked out the back of the house. I followed him into this empty field, where he began teaching me how to shoot and how to throw a punch." Cassie smiled at the memory. "I can hold my own because of him."

"It sounds like he was a good man," Ryan said, rising to take his turn.

"He was."

Above them, a door opened, and Duke leaped off the thick rug and ran up the stairs with lightning speed, his nails skidding on the vinyl floor at the top.

"Kate's home," Ryan said.

Cassie knew it was her decision to be here, but her stomach still twisted.

"Are you coming?" Ryan asked.

"Be right there," Cassie said, while Ryan disappeared up the stairs. She took her time putting away the darts and stopped in front of a painted wooden nativity set Kate had displayed on a bookshelf. *Lord, I hope coming here was the right choice. Please, watch over our steps and our decisions.* A bubbly female laugh floated down from the kitchen, pulling Cassie's gaze upward. Right or wrong, they were here now. Cassie sighed and flicked off the basement lights. Whatever happened next, good or bad, she would figure out a way to deal with it.

Rounding the corner into the kitchen, Cassie almost bumped into Ryan. He was hugging a woman she assumed was Kate. But the way he was looking at her made Cassie wonder: What exactly was the history between the two of them?

Ryan stepped aside and beamed down at the woman beside him, his arm comfortably resting on her shoulder. "Kate, this is Cassie. The one I've told you about."

In her mind's eye, Cassie had thought Kate would be tall, but she barely brushed Ryan's shoulder in height. She seemed better suited to being a horse jockey than an FBI agent. Kate extended her hand toward Cassie, the woman's dark brown eyes holding an air of challenge.

"Nice to meet you," Kate said, her smile almost reaching her eyes.

Cassie shook her hand but couldn't ignore the feeling that coming here was a mistake.

Not one to be forgotten, Duke pushed into the middle of them, whining at their feet. "All right, Duke," Kate said and reached behind her into one of the grocery bags on the kitchen counter. The rustling sack perked the dog's ears, and he nearly shimmied out of his skin when Kate pulled out a bone. She gave a signal, and Duke did a series of tricks, finishing by rolling over.

"Good dog," Kate said and dropped the rawhide. Like a hawk, Duke snapped it up and whisked his treasure to a corner of the living room, noisily gnawing on it.

"It's been way too long," Ryan said.

"It has, but there is a cure for that," Kate said, jabbing at his ribs. "It's called picking up the phone."

While Cassie didn't doubt that FBI partners shared a bond, something unspoken between the two of them made her heart clench. Over the years, Ryan had barely mentioned Kate. Now, watching them together made her wonder why that was. She had assumcd it was because they were merely partners, not friends, but that obviously was not the case.

"Shall I put some coffee on?" Kate asked, her hands already in the process.

"You read my mind," Ryan said and found a seat at the pine table. While the coffee perked, Ryan began asking after people at the FBI and Kate happily answered. The conversation quickly swung to new policies and politics going on within their old team.

Cassie wandered over to the counter and began looking over the groceries that sat as neglected as she felt. She lifted out a variety of fresh vegetables, herbs and steaks, laying them out on the small workspace. Her mind started mulling over different recipes. "Why don't I start dinner?" she said.

"That's okay. I've got it," Kate replied.

"Honestly, I'd let her," Ryan said, halting Kate in her tracks. "Cassie's restaurant is legendary. Customers travel for miles to eat her cooking."

"A *chef*?" Kate stated, raising a skeptical eyebrow.

"Yes. WITSEC wouldn't allow me to continue as an artist. So I fell back on my other skill set, cooking. My grandmother was a caterer, and my brothers and I would often help out. I always say I learned from the best," Cassie replied.

The wind blustered outside, sending hard plaits of freezing rain against the window beside the door.

A tight smile stretched across Kate's face. *"Mi casa es su casa."*

Happy to do something with her hands, Cassie ignored Kate's attitude as she showed her where the spices, knives and pots were. Setting to work, Cassie began vigorously chopping, feeling more in her element.

"So, can you bring us up-to-date on The Wolf?" Ryan asked while Kate topped up her coffee and stuck in a candy cane. Ryan pulled a face. "That's ghastly," he said.

Kate just smiled and swirled her coffee with the candy. "We haven't learned much more since Cassie went into WITSEC," Kate said, blowing on her drink. "The Wolf works as an assassin for hire, sometimes alone, sometimes with a hired crew." She nodded at Cassie. "Your sketches and paintings are still the only images we have of him."

Cassie tossed onions into the pan, sending up a loud, caramelizing sizzle. "Weren't they stolen?"

Kate's mug stopped halfway to her mouth. "How do you know that?"

"The Wolf." Saying his name sent a shiver down her spine. Cassie shook it off, added more vegetables to the onions and set the steaks in a separate skillet. "He told me he has them hanging in his home."

A heavy knock thumped at the door, making everyone jump, including Duke. Instantly Ryan moved for his weapon, but Kate calmly placed her hand on his shoulder. Walking to the door, she looked out the peephole. "It's Agents Thomas and Bell," she said and, without explanation, slipped outside.

"Who are they, and why are they here?" Cassie asked accusingly.

Ryan's face hardened. "I don't know."

When Kate came back in, she was soaked right through, her dark bobbed hair dripping down her face. "That storm is nasty out there," she said, pulling a tea towel from the drawer and dabbing at her cheeks.

"Why are they here?" Cassie barked.

Instead of answering, Kate sat at the table. She folded the towel neatly and set it before her while her face went professionally blank. Kate raised her eyes and leveled a look at Cassie that made her want to run.

"The Marshals are hunting everywhere for you."

Of course, they would be, Cassie thought. She was the district attorney's star witness against The Wolf if they ever found him. And that was a big *if.*

Kate swung her eyes to Ryan.

His jaw tightened. "You told the FBI that I was bringing her here."

"Walter authorized a small protective detail. It's just Agents Thomas and Bell. One car. That's it."

Ryan's eyes narrowed with disgust. "I can't believe you would betray us like this."

"Betray you? You're asking me to single-handedly protect a valuable asset from one of the world's deadliest assassins. I can't do that on my own, and you know it." She matched his glower. "It's a wonder this place isn't swarming with law enforcement. The Marshals are practically turning over every rock in the state of Oregon to find her. I have used every favor I have—and I mean, *every* favor—to keep this operation as low-key as possible."

"I trusted you," Ryan said, pushing away from the table.

Her mind reeling, Cassie focused on cooking. They couldn't force her back into WITSEC, could they? She added herbs to the pan. Ryan and Kate bickered in the background, but she heard none of it. Methodically, Cassie plated and began serving the food. The lights flickered, and she barely registered the worsening storm.

She set her plate on the table, her chair screeching on the floor as she sat down. The most important thing was to stay calm. Kate was doing her job, what she was designed to do. She wouldn't have broken Ryan's trust lightly.

At that moment, Cassie felt God's warning. There was more going on here, and they all needed to understand precisely what that was.

Cassie took a deep breath and turned to Ryan. "Could you please say grace?" Ryan's mouth twisted in surprise. She could tell he didn't want to, but it was precisely what he needed to do. "Please," Cassie said. "I would really like to eat."

He looked like he was about to say something but instead bent his head respectfully. The prayer was only a quick blessing over the food, but it was enough to bridle his temper.

Deliberately, Cassie ignored the tension at the table, cutting into her steak, and said, "I've been in protective custody before. This doesn't feel like a handoff from the FBI to the Marshals."

Kate's back stiffened. "Because it's not," she said. "The Marshals are not aware that you are here...yet."

"What are you playing at?" Ryan growled.

"The Marshals want Cassie back in their custody for obvious reasons. However, the FBI would like her to consider remaining in theirs."

"Why?" Ryan bit out. Cassie put a silencing hand on his knee.

"My friend at the US Marshals' office leaked some information to me that I shared with our boss at the FBI." Ignoring her food, Kate leaned forward across the table, focusing solely on Cassie. "When you phoned your control agent, an alert was sent out, and a team of marshals were dispatched to your house to check on things. Did you tell Ryan what happened at your place, what sent you running?"

Cassie closed her eyes. "No."

Kate swiveled in her chair, turning to Ryan. "You remember The White Rose Serial Killer case we worked on?"

"We were never able to close it, so of course I remember. What has that got to do with anything?"

"Tell me if this sounds familiar," Kate said patiently. "The screen from Cassie's bedroom window was removed, the clothes in her dresser drawers were perfectly arranged and dusted with white rose petals."

Ryan's eyes rounded.

"In the garage, the Marshals found Cassie's paint studio with a canvas that had been painted over with the words, 'Ordained with pure white roses, their scent sweet upon your skin—'"

Ryan's voice took over. "'Ardor long last requited, love forever bound herein.'"

Cassie felt her appetite disappear as she looked at Ryan questioningly. "How do you know that?"

"It's half of a poem. We're not sure if he wrote it or someone else," Ryan said. He leaned back in his chair, stunned. "And they are the words and actions of The White Rose Serial Killer." He wiped his hand over his face. "He stalked Cassie on her walk home. All the hallmarks are there."

"What are you guys talking about? The man who was chasing me is The Wolf. I saw him."

The color drained from Ryan's face. "When I showed up at your house, The Wolf must have been there. I interfered with his plan. That must be why the alarm went off at my house. He tripped it to get me out of the way."

"Hello?" Cassie rapped her knuckles on the table. "I'm not understanding."

Ryan's eyes went blank as the information fell into place. "But you showed up at my house, and The Wolf wasn't expecting that. When we were in the backyard, the way we were standing, he couldn't shoot me without risking hurting you. He toyed with Logan hoping to draw me out, to kill me, but you're an excellent shot."

Cassie jolted when Kate touched her wrist, drawing her attention.

"When Ryan and I were partners, The White Rose Serial Killer case came across our desk. His MO is always the same. He stalks his victims at night when they're walking home from something. We believe he does it to heighten their sense of fear since he never attacks when they're out in the open. He waits until the victim is sleeping, then he infiltrates their homes through their bedroom window. We always find the victim's place left in immaculate condition with white rose petals in their dresser drawers and always, somewhere in the house, we find the poem. The victim is typically held hostage for a few days in another location before being discovered strangled and arranged in a public garden covered in white roses. So far, there are only three known kills in the United States—one in Oregon, one in Tennessee and one in New York. His victims are all attractive females and each very talented in their field of work."

Cassie's pulse thundered in her ears. She looked over at Ryan, but his attention remained squarely on Kate. "We've never had any reason to suspect that The Wolf and The White Rose Serial Killer were the same man."

"We didn't," Kate admitted and squeezed Cassie's hand. "That's why you're so important. You're not only a witness to The Wolf's assassination of the congressman, but you're also the only link that proves that The White Rose Serial Killer and The Wolf are one person."

Not hungry anymore, Cassie pushed away from the table. She stood at the kitchen counter and stared blankly at the wall in front of her. This was a lot of information to digest.

"The Marshals want to put you back into WITSEC," Kate said. "But, Cassie, the FBI wants to give you a choice. It's been eight years, and we haven't gotten close to The Wolf or The White Rose Serial Killer. Until now, we believed you were just another name on The Wolf's hit list. Someonc that he would eventually come after. But in the last few hours, that's all changed. We know that you are more than just a name to him. He's obsessed with you. Understanding that gives us an advantage."

"No!" Ryan thundered. "I see where you are heading with this, and I don't like it."

"The Wolf is smart," Kate pointed out, "and he's coming after Cassie, whether she stays in WITSEC or leaves it." Kate met Cassie's eyes. "My team at the FBI wants you in their custody. Please, don't misunderstand me, we will do everything to minimize your risk, but we want to leverage the fact that an attack upon you is imminent. We want to have a team poised to strike back when The Wolf makes his move against you. Ryan is right. There would be some danger, but staying with the Marshals who haven't been successful in hiding you isn't without risk either. The Wolf is coming after you. That is a fact. Why not have a team of trained FBI agcnts watching your back, ready to take him out when he makes his move?"

Kate's offer was terrifying, but Cassie could see it for what it truly was: an answer to her prayer for direction. Ryan would want her to choose the Marshals and the new identity they'd offer her along with a new life in a new state. If she trusted the Marshals, that move would make sense. However, if The Wolf could get to Gerald, he could get to anyone. Simply relocating would only be a repeat of what happened in Bakerton, and next time, she might not escape. Kate was right. The Wolf was coming after her no matter what. The real question was, who did she trust to keep her safe? There was only one answer to that—the FBI.

The room was quiet, and then, as if on cue, thunder crashed and the lights flickered again, sending Duke howling down the hallway.

Ryan scowled at Kate, his jaw clenched. He looked like a caged tiger waiting to pounce, and Cassie just didn't have the heart for it. Words wouldn't change what had to be done. What she needed was a moment to pray about her next steps. "I'm going to grab a sweater from my bag," she said and retreated from the room. Her feet had barely reached the hall when she heard their hushed voices talking about her.

In the guest room, Cassie searched through the duffel and pulled out her sweater. She sat, deflated, on the edge of the bed and contemplated what she would say to Ryan. The lights surged with brightness, sputtered and then cut out, shrouding the room in shadows and blanketing the house in silence. The hairs on the back of her neck bristled. She leaned out the guest room door and found Kate garbed in a parka, rummaging through a closet halfway down the hall.

"Is everything all right?" Cassie asked.

"I know I've got some candles in here somewhere," Kate said, reaching blindly into the back of the closet. She passed a flashlight to Cassie. "Can you shine that in here for me?" Kate stretched to her full height and pawed back a little farther. "Here we are," she said, pulling out two chunky white pillar candles. "Agents Thomas and Bell are checking out the power situation, but until we get the all clear, I'd like you to stay in the kitchen."

Cassie's spine tightened. "You think this is The Wolf?"

"I'm not sure, and until I am, we need to be cautious," Kate said, passing her the candles and taking back the flashlight. She met Cassie's eye with a look that kept her still. "Before we head back in there, I need to ask you something, and it's going to seem forward."

Cassie raised an eyebrow.

"What's the deal between you and Ryan?"

"Excuse me?" Cassie sputtered.

"I need to know where Ryan's head is at when it comes to you. Are you two dating?"

"No," Cassie said. "No. Not at all. We had a relationship, but it didn't work out."

"It's over between the two of you."

Cassie looked past Kate's shoulder toward the kitchen. "It is," she said, more definitively than she felt. "Ryan's here only because he thinks he owes me, and you know how he is."

A slow smile spread across Kate's face. "That I do. All too well."

Together, they reentered the kitchen just as Ryan turned on a small battery-powered lantern in the middle of the table. Soft yellow light lit up the room, setting eerie shadows about the corners. His hand went to the police radio unit in front of him. "Hey, Kate, what channel are you guys on?"

"We're on four," Kate replied, passing Cassie a lighter from the drawer. Her hand deliberately brushed Cassie's arm, and she whispered, "Don't let him talk you into anything."

Cassie looked at her quizzically.

"See you guys in a bit," Kate said, unholstering her gun. "I'm going to help the boys outside complete their check. It's not often we get thundersnow."

Cassie lit the candles and set them on the

back counter. "She seems oddly happy to be going out in this."

"Kate is quite the outdoorswoman." Ryan pulled out the chair beside him. "Why don't you come and sit down."

She stared at the seat. "Because something tells me I'm not going to like what you have to say."

"Please."

Cassie sighed and moved into the chair beside him. She glanced at the window. The blinds were now closed, but the snow was coming down so hard it sounded like rain against the glass. Outdoorswoman or not, if she were Kate, she would have chosen to be outside over being a part of this conversation too.

Ryan eyed her carefully. "I want you to consider staying in WITSEC."

Cassie's jaw clenched.

"Kate makes the FBI sound like a sure thing," Ryan said, taking her hand in his, "but they can't make any guarantees on how things will turn out. They have lost good, trained agents to The Wolf."

"So have the Marshals," she said, thinking of Gerald.

"They have," he agreed. "We all have. But the Marshals are good at what they do. I'm worried that because of what happened in Bakerton, you're not able to see that."

His thumb rubbed the palm of her hand—something he used to do when they were dating. Her gaze lowered to their entwined hands, suddenly feeling the depth of how much she missed this closeness with him.

"Once you leave the program, there's no guarantee they'll take you back. All I'm asking," Ryan's eyes implored, "is that you don't rush into this decision."

"Time is a luxury I don't have. For all we know, The Wolf has already found us. At best, I have until morning."

The police radio squelched to life. "All clear. It looks like the power outage is from the storm."

Cassie took a breath and pulled her hand from Ryan's. It had been a long forty-eight hours, and his touch was clouding her judgment. "I'm really drained. If there's no danger," she said, pushing back from the table, "I'm going to turn in." Without meeting his eye, Cassie rose quickly and retreated to the guest bedroom before he could argue.

Rattled by her growing feelings for Ryan, she lifted her duffel bag off the floor and onto the bed when something hard clamped over her mouth. Cassie savagely slammed her elbow into the body of her attacker. The man threw her facedown onto the bed, his forceful hand grabbing her head and suffocating her in the thick duvet. She thrashed against the immovable force, her lungs screaming for air.

"Shhh," he whispered, letting her take one greedy breath whilc his knee dug into her spine. "It'll hurt less if you stay still." She felt a sharp pinch in the side of her neck, and suddenly, everything faded to black.

SEVEN

Ryan knocked on Cassie's bedroom door with a tea in hand, the morning light streaming in the window at the end of the hall. He'd been wrong about a lot of things lately, and he was brave enough to admit it, but not about WITSEC. The thought of something going wrong, of Cassie in the hands of The Wolf, left a sinking sensation in his stomach.

He knocked again on the door. No answer.

"Cassie, I've got tea," he said, listening intently. There were no annoyed groans, no sound of tired feet moving across the floor, nothing. His gut twisted. He set the tea down on a console table and knocked louder. Kate appeared in the hallway. "Cassie, if you don't say something, I'm going to come in." He exchanged a worried look with Kate and then barged into the room. His eyes darted from the bed, to the floor, to the window. It felt like the room was swallowing him whole. There was no Cassie. Only a dropped syringe, a white rose and an open window with blowing curtains.

"I'm going to call this in," Kate said.

He touched her wrist. "I won't be shut out of this investigation."

"I'll try my best, but you're too close to this one."

Ryan rubbed his eyes. He stared out the fourth-story window of the FBI field office in Portland. The midmorning sun filtered through the mini-blinds but did nothing to warm the conference room or his heart. His mind kept replaying Kate's security cam footage of a man approaching the rear of her house from the river. A bold move in the dark with a storm raging. The image of the male was too grainy for a positive identification, even with the FBI's world-class technology, but none of the federal agents doubted that it was The Wolf. Only an assassin as highly trained as The Wolf could pull off an abduction like that.

The door opened, and Ryan looked up. Special agent in charge, Walter Dunlack, marched in like the bulldog he was. What Walter lacked in height, he made up for in presence. His round, bald head and large jowls reminded Ryan of Sir Winston Churchill. If only the similarities extended beyond that, then maybe his old boss would have made a good leader.

Walter sat across the table from Ryan. "I should charge you with obstruction for the way you've handled this," he said. "But, for old time's sake, I'm not going to. However, I expect that you will stay out of this investigation. Bccause, trust me, if you so much as sneeze in the way of this case, I will have you hauled up on charges faster than you can spit."

"Come on. I'm too involved in this for you to freeze me out now." Ryan glared.

"You know the rules. Cassie is your girlfriend."

"She's my *ex*-girlfriend and has been for almost a year. I'm a decorated agent, and I have a deep understanding of all the players involved. I'm an asset, and you know it."

Walter leaned back in his chair, making the springs groan in protest. "The FBI is not a revolving door, my friend. You don't get to play small-town police officer one minute and an FBI agent when it suits you." Walter looked at him shrewdly. "We've been talking for months about you coming back. Consider this decision time. Either you join my team permanently or not at all."

And there it was, Walter's underhanded play.

Ryan shook his head and stared up at the

ceiling, concealing his thunderous thoughts; trust Walter to leverage a situation like this. There was nothing he wouldn't do to be on the FBI team looking for Cassie, but there was a steep cost to remaining an agent beyond that. In the beginning, Ryan had loved working for the FBI, and he was good at it. He enjoyed hunting monsters. Nothing compared to the adrenaline rush of putting evil behind bars, but over time it had taken a toll. Especially when he lost; when he couldn't get enough evidence to catch the killer before they struck again. There were no second chances in this line of work and being one of the best investigators didn't mean much when you couldn't save them all.

Walter rose from his chair. "Well, if that's your answer, don't forget to leave your visitor's badge at the front desk on your way out."

"Wait," Ryan said. "Will you guarantee that I'll be on this case?"

"I'll let you stay on the periphery of it, but that's it."

"I can live with that," Ryan said, blinking back his anger. "Now, why don't you fill me in on what the team has come up with?"

Sitting back down, Walter leaned forward. "The tox screen on the syringe you found at Kate's has come back in. We've confirmed that Cassie was drugged with a heavy sedative, and we have good reason to believe that she's still alive."

"What else?"

"You're familiar with the rest area beside the Halsey Bridge just north of Kate's place?" Ryan nodded. "This morning, agents discovered a small fishing pontoon boat abandoned on its shores, and we caught a break. Some bird-watchers had set up a couple of webcams in the bridge's upper girders. The footage isn't great, but we think we can place The Wolf coming down the river at about 9:30 p.m., and then at about 9:45 p.m., a silver Volvo with one burned-out headlight crosses the bridge."

"The Wolf?"

"Or coincidence, we can't say for certain."

Something stirred within Ryan. "Can I see the footage of that and for the nearby highways?"

Walter looked at him skeptically. "The team assigned has come up with nothing. There's no proof it's The Wolf driving that car. I'd be sending you on a wild-goose chase."

"It keeps me out of your hair."

"Not that I have much of that," Walter said, picking up the conference room phone and calling IT.

Birds chirped loudly. The noise stabbed through Cassie's temple like an ice pick. She pulled her pillow over her ears and felt the scratchy mattress beneath her. *Where am I?* Her thoughts quickly flew to her last memory, sending her heart slamming into her chest. She jumped up from the bed, making her head pound even harder. The sound of metal scraping against metal and a tug on her lower calf forced her to sit back down. *What's on my leg?* Cassie's hands moved to her left ankle and ran over the metal cuff that chained her to a handrail bolted to an adjacent wall near the floor. She pulled against the restraint, only to hear the metal links sing against each other. Her eyes widened with panic. Instinctually, she yanked and thrashed the chain to no avail.

Cassie sank onto the edge of the mattress, feeling defeated and praying for calm. Memories of last night—of Ryan's hand in hers—flitted through her mind. She took a deep breath. If Ryan were here, what would he do? Cassie looked around her. He would break the situation down into facts.

So what did she know? She was in a large rectangular bedroom. The walls were bare, and the only furnishings besides the antique iron bed was a small round table. Cassie got up, tested how far she could walk and found that she could move fairly freely about the room. Just not close enough to reach the interior door on one side of the room or the window on the opposite wall. She stared again at the window. The blinds were beyond her reach and tilted just enough to allow light in, but perfectly angled so that the outside world remained obscured.

The door creaked, and Cassie spun around. The Wolf stood in the open doorway to her room, his hands laden with a tray and a canvas.

Her heart locked in terror. She looked to the exterior window but knew it offered no escape. Her gaze flew back to his. *Get it together, Cassie,* she thought to herself, *or he's going to kill you.* A slow smile spread across The Wolf's face.

"Where am I?" Cassie demanded, standing tall.

"Such a typical question. Do you really think I'm going to answer that?"

"No."

"Well then," he said, putting the tray and canvas on the table and standing back, "come and look. I brought you an early Christmas gift."

Cassie didn't move. Her pulse thundered in her ears, but she held her ground.

The Wolf tutted his tongue. "You're a smart girl," he said. "It's one of the things I admire about you. Don't make this difficult on yourself."

Cassie thought about charging him, about lashing out, but where would that get her? She was as much a captive as any inmate held in a high-security prison. Pushing down the hollow feeling inside, Cassie walked toward the table but remained silent.

"I understand your disdain," he said, his voice soft. "It took far longer to find you than even I expected. Maybe you thought that I didn't appreciate your sketches of me?" He moved to stand beside her. "Or that I wasn't looking for you at all? Please, don't be mad." The Wolf stroked her cheek. "The Marshals stole you away from me. But I made it my mission to find you, my sweet."

"I'm not your sweet." Cassie swiped his hand from her face, and just as quickly he grabbed her wrist.

"You're trying to provoke me," he said, malice flashing in his eyes. "I'll advise you not to do that. I'd prefer not to rush our time together." His gaze softened. "Come, now. Let's look at what I brought you."

On the table was a beautiful set of art brushes with high-quality paints, but she wasn't going to tell him that. "What do you want from me?"

He took pictures from his coat pocket and set them on the table. “Your next masterpieces.”

Cassie twisted away, but he gripped the nape of her neck and forced her to look.

The top photo wasn’t as awful as she had expected. It was of a young woman. Her long, dark brown hair lay outstretched around her, with perfect white roses entwined within it. She lay artfully posed on the ground in a garden. The woman looked peaceful, like she had decided to take an unexpected nap.

“Beautiful, isn’t it,” The Wolf said, breaking into Cassie’s thoughts.

“Is she dead?”

“Yes.” A smile turned the corners of his lips. “She was the first that I set free from this earth.”

Cassie struggled for words over the knot in her throat. There were far more than three photos in the stack. How many women had he killed that the FBI didn’t know about? “Who is she?” Cassie asked, wanting to gather as much information as she could.

“Olivia Cosay,” he said, tenderly touching the edges of the photo.

The name didn’t ring any bells for Cassie, but to someone, this girl was family. “I don’t understand how you can be The Wolf and then do something like this? One murder so callous and the other…”

He shrugged. "Everyone has to pay the bills," he said, "but these girls are my loves." A brilliant smile spread across his face as he looked to Cassie. "I want you to paint them for me."

"No." The word came out before she thought about it.

"Don't be jealous," The Wolf threatened when his cell phone rang. He looked down at the number and sighed. "It's work." He turned to leave but stopped in the doorway. "I will be back, Cassie," he said pointedly. "Behave until then."

She ran at him, but her leg shackle made her come up short. The Wolf just chuckled and closed the door behind him. Within moments, an engine sputtered to life and took off down the driveway.

Ryan noted that it was starting to get dark as he flicked on the windshield wipers and cleared off the dusting of snowflakes. He sighed. Part of him worried that this was a fool's errand, but something in his gut assured him it wasn't. During his search of the highway cam footage, he had discovered the gray Volvo with one burned-out headlight near Frog Lake on Highway 26. Then through various cameras, Ryan had followed the car on its journey south until it turned off in the small city of Pine Springs. While there was no way to know for sure who the driver of the Volvo was, Ryan felt certain it was The Wolf.

He parked his unmarked car in the parking lot at Hanley's and stepped out, filling his lungs with crisp winter air. The last grocery store on his list had turned up nothing. Coming here, a gas station with a small mini-mart attached, was a last-ditch effort. He didn't have much hope for a lead, but he had time to kill before hitting the town diners during dinner rush and asking questions there.

Ryan glanced at his watch. His throat tightened. Yesterday, at this very moment, he'd been playing darts with Cassie. Ryan pushed his thoughts to the back of his brain. He needed to focus. The longest The White Rose Serial Killer had kept anyone alive was five days.

Ryan pulled open the spotless glass door, setting off an electronic beep that produced a teenage clerk from the cooler.

"Can I help you?" the young man asked.

"I hope you can." Ryan pulled out his badge, and the boy's eyes grew big. "I'm looking for someone." He produced a replica of the sketch Cassie had done of The Wolf all those years ago. "Have you seen anyone that looks like this man? He may have altered his appearance some."

"No, can't say as I have," the boy said.

"Anything unusual or out of the normal routine happen in the last few days? Even if it seems unimportant," Ryan asked patiently. "Sometimes, the smallest things can break a case."

The boy's lips twisted while he thought. "Well," he said, "it's probably nothing. But the only thing that's been odd is Peggy."

"Peggy?"

"Ya, Peggy has a nice cottage out near the Deschutes River. Mostly rents it out in the summer, but occasionally in the off-season, she'll rent it out for longer. When that happens, Peggy usually pops into the store after she does a walk through with a tenant. She drops off a spare set of keys and has me keep an eye on the place. She lives over in Bend, and it's a pain for her to get over here all the time."

Ryan narrowed his eyes. "Keep an eye on the place? What does that mean?"

"You know, she slips me some cash, and if something goes wrong maintenance-wise, I take care of it. They call her, and she calls me. Anyways, she stopped in the store before she went up there to show the place on Monday, and she never came back to drop off the spare keys or cash."

"Maybe she didn't rent it out."

The boy shook his head. "She must've because Fred has seen a car come and go from her place."

"Did he happen to tell you what type of car?"

"I believe it was some sort of Volvo."

"Can you jot down that address? I think I'd like to check that out."

Cassie stared at the handrail, getting down on all fours to look at how it was anchored to the wall. There had to be some way of getting out of this, she thought, but nothing she had done so far had worked. *God, what am I supposed to do?* Disheartened, Cassie sat on the floor and leaned against the bed, her spine striking the metal from the side rail.

A thought ignited.

She sprang to her feet and pushed the mattresses onto the floor. Her eyes riveted to the two iron tongue-and-groove side rails that held the foot-and headboards in place. Wasting no time, Cassie yanked on one of the bars until it clattered onto the floor, then carried it over to the handrail. With a determined heave, she jabbed her makeshift tool into the floor between the wall and the rail. Her hands slid to the top of her pry-bar, and she worked it back and forth until screws began to pop and the handrail fell onto the hardwood.

Heart racing, Cassie slid off the part of her leg shackle that was attached to the rail. The other half of the restraint was still around her ankle, but there was no time to deal with that. Instead, she shoved the photos into her jeans pocket and bolted for the door, the chain trailing noisily after her.

When she reached the end of the hall, Cassie didn't stop. She saw the outside door on the other side of the living room and charged. Her fingers flew to the locks, and the door swung open. Excited, Cassie leaped out onto the cement front stoop when burning cold stabbed through her bare feet, making her scramble back inside.

The door stood open before her, and frustrated tears sprang to her eyes. All she could see beyond the house's clearing was trees, upon trees, upon trees. Her stomach sank. She was in the middle of nowhere with darkness settling in, and temperatures that would soon be dropping. She wasn't a fool. Eyeing the snow, Cassie knew hypothermia was as real a threat as The Wolf.

She retreated into the house, and glanced around the living room, looking for anything that could help her. Cassie's gaze froze. Just above the arm of an overstuffed sofa, she could see tufts of curly, white hair. Her heart thudded. Slowly, Cassie rose onto her tiptoes, peering over the back of the couch. An older woman lay there, perfectly still.

"Hello?" Cassie said.

There was no response.

Cassie moved beside her, saying a quiet prayer. She brushed aside the gold chain at the woman's neck that read 'Peggy,' and checked for a pulse. The woman's chilled skin spoke the answer before her lack of a beating heart did. Cassie let out a silent scream.

She had to get out of here. Her eyes locked onto a closet. Ripping it open, she discovered a large pair of men's boots along with a heavy-weight flannel coat. Good enough. Cassie plunged into the winter gear and raced out the door. Her feet slid awkwardly inside the over-size boots, making her more stumble than run down the front flight of steps.

She darted down the snowplowed driveway as a gray Volvo started to turn in. Quickly she veered off toward the protection of the trees, deftly ducking into them. Had he seen her? Cassie ran, her boots crunching loudly through the wet snow until she popped out where the trees bordered the road. She looked as far as she could in both directions, hoping to see smoke from a chimney or a plowed driveway, but there was nothing except wilderness. Her chest tightened, the cold air stinging the back of her throat. There wasn't a single clue as to which way held civilization and which led her deeper into the snarling forest.

A whine from an engine blared to life. Cassie froze. The sound was coming from the direction of the cottage.

With her heart beating wildly, she ran back into the woods that bordered the line of the road. She darted between the trees, but the ground began descending into a slushy, wet mess. It sucked at her huge boots, making her feet slide inside them, slowing her down. Her pulse hammered in her ears. She recognized that engine sound now. An ATV was maneuvering through the woods, stopping and starting, probably searching for her tracks in the dark.

She pushed herself to move faster, but without streetlights, night was falling hard, making it more difficult by the second to see where she was going. Cassie glanced over her shoulder.

A light was darting between the trees. Suddenly, it steadied, and the ATV's engine began to rev with a challenge.

Run.

Cassie's muscles, cold and tired, didn't want

to cooperate. Her mind was moving much faster than her limbs, filling her with panic. She scurried awkwardly up an embankment and across the road into the woods on the other side.

The ATV engine roared louder. Suddenly, a spotlight lit up the world around her. Her shadow now lay in front of her on the white, glittering snow. There was no way she could outrun an ATV. Cassie spotted some denser brush and darted toward it, hoping to force him off his vehicle.

A shot blasted into the night, tearing a whimper from her lips.

Cassie looked behind her when she slipped on some ice, sending her careening over a fallen log. Her shin burned, and then she was rolling, rolling down a hill. Sticks tore at her flesh while rocks pounded her head and back. In a battered mess, her body stopped at the bottom of the slope. She lay perfectly still, the world spinning around her.

A spotlight began darting in an irregular pattern over the ground. Somewhere, Cassie registered that she should get up and move, but her limbs lay motionless.

The light landed on her. So bright.

She closed her eyes, turned her head and vomited in the snow.

Footsteps thumped down the hill.

"Why do you insist on doing things the hard way?" The Wolf asked.

The road had been long and winding, making Ryan thankful when the GPS said he had arrived at his destination. It was one of a handful of cottages located on this side of the Deschutes River. It was supposed to be the second phase of a planned resort community, but when the economy had turned sour, people had stopped buying, and this half of the development lay deserted and abandoned.

He parked his car across the end of a long driveway, thankful for the trees that obscured his vehicle from the cottage. Noting the recently plowed drive, Ryan moved cautiously toward the house with his flashlight tucked down. Cassie was here. He could feel it in his bones.

Ryan rounded the bend and flicked off his flashlight. A white cottage stood in a small clearing, with a dim glow coming from around the edges of its closed blinds. The yard, blanketed in white, looked clean of debris except for an old farm tractor parked near the house. Off to the right stood a detached wooden garage that looked like it had been built as an afterthought. Ryan pulled his gun from its holster and crept over to the garage. Quietly, he moved down the side of the building and found an old single-paned window next to the side access door. Rubbing the frost off the glass, he shone his flashlight inside—a silver Volvo.

A loud screech came from the house. Ryan sunk low, put his back to the garage and slid to the corner of the building. From this vantage point, he could see the cottage's back door where an ATV sat parked near its steps.

Something was up, and whatever it was, Ryan felt confident that it was nothing good. He studied the cottage, but there were no obvious signs of what was going on inside the house. What he needed was to get a closer look. Ryan kept low, then dashed behind an overturned aluminum boat not far from the garage.

The back door light flicked on, making Ryan's breath catch. He gripped his gun tighter, ready for whatever came next.

The Wolf materialized at the top of the back steps. He cast a stony glance over the clearing, then warily grabbed a jerrican off the ATV rack and disappeared back into the house.

Ryan fought to remain where he was. Part of him wanted to bury every last bullet he had into The Wolf, but what if Cassie wasn't inside the house? What then? He felt sick to his stomach, knowing a dead Wolf couldn't talk.

He ducked down and darted back to the side of the garage and pulled his cell phone from his pocket. Before he could change his mind, he began dialing.

"Special Agent Dunlack," Walter said briskly.

"It's Ryan. I was right about Pine Springs. The Wolf is here."

"What's your location?"

"4209 East Deschutes Road."

There was a muffle of voices, and then Walter spoke again. "We're thirty minutes out by chopper. I'm contacting local authorities for quicker assistance. Hold your position until they arrive."

The large metal garage door whined open. Ryan peered around the corner. The Wolf was advancing toward him, past the old tractor, each shoulder harboring large duffel bags.

"I don't think that's going to be possible. The Wolf's on the move," Ryan said, cutting off the call. He scooted back along the wall and expected the side access door to be locked, but it opened easily. Adrenaline, coupled with controlled rage, coursed through his veins as he threw open the door and yelled, "FBI. Freeze."

Visibly shocked, The Wolf purposefully dropped the bags at the rear of the car.

"Well, look who's stopped by for a visit. Ryan, isn't it?"

Ryan steadied his gun on The Wolf. "Hands in the air, turn around and on your knees."

The Wolf didn't move. "Did you like the drive out here?" he asked. "Personally, I enjoy the woods. And out here, it feels like they're never-ending."

"I said, hands in the air and on your knees."

The Wolf sighed. "You feds are no fun at all." With slow robotic movements, he dropped first to one knee and then the other.

"Hands in the air!" Ryan yelled, shaking his gun.

Rolling his eyes, The Wolf raised his arms, and Ryan cautiously stepped forward.

"You probably think Cassie's here, don't you?"

A drop of fear slid into Ryan's stomach, threatening to ignite, but he kept his face neutral.

The Wolf ran his tongue over his teeth, his eyes turning dark. "You do, don't you?" He laughed. "Why would I keep Cassie here, in a place that is so warm and comfortable?" His eyes closed thoughtfully. "That just wouldn't do. Women are always more cooperative when they want something. Tell me, Ryan, how long do you think it'll take before Cassie freezes to death out there?" He exhaled, letting his breath turn into a white vapor. "It's very cold out tonight."

"Shut up and get on your belly," Ryan snarled through gritted teeth. The Wolf didn't move, and Ryan took one step closer. "I said—"

With lightning speed, The Wolf leaped toward Ryan's gun, knocking it into the air. A bullet pinged wildly off metal, ricocheting through the garage. Brutally, The Wolf slammed into Ryan's chest, stealing his breath and toppling them both onto the ground. Locked together, the two rolled on the dirt floor. Ryan struggled to deliver more blows than he received, but The Wolf was a well-trained fighter. Blood dripped into Ryan's eye when sirens began to blare in the distance. With a well-placed kick, Ryan knocked The Wolf off of him.

"Where is Cassie?" Ryan said, throwing a punch. The Wolf twisted and rolled over the trunk of the car, his hands pulling a gun from a bag on the far side that Ryan hadn't seen.

Scrambling for cover, Ryan ducked behind a metal workbench. The Wolf fired rapid successive shots, keeping Ryan pinned, while he backed toward a woodpile that lined the edge of the garage.

Hunkered low, Ryan noticed his gun lying exposed on the dirt floor. He reached for the weapon when a gunshot exploded a jerrican of fuel next to the woodpile. A whoosh of flames devoured the dry wood. The fire spread quickly, licking up the walls and shedding an oppressive heat that squeezed Ryan's lungs, making him choke for air. He had to find Cassie.

Gaining his footing, Ryan raced out of the garage. The Wolf had almost reached the ATV. There was no way he was lctting The Wolf escape, not when Cassie's life hung in the balance. With cold efficiency, Ryan dropped to his knee, leveled his gun and fired. The shot missed, but The Wolf changed direction and dove behind the old John Deere tractor.

Ryan realized he was exposed and flattened to the ground, rolling back behind the overturned aluminum fishing boat.

"You've got nowhere to run," Ryan yelled.

"That's okay. I'm happy to sit here. We can listen together as our girl burns."

Ryan's heart clenched in his chest.

"You're lying. You said she was in the woods."

"Was I lying then, or am I now?" The Wolf extended his hand, and Ryan heard the car locks click into place. "It's impossible to know for sure, but I'm telling you, she's in that trunk. Can't say that I'll promise to wait while you check."

The heat from the fire burned hot against Ryan's back.

"You can have the girl or you can have me, but you can't have both."

Ryan squeezed his eyes shut. He couldn't risk it. Carefully, he retreated backward into the garage.

The ATV revved to life while Ryan took a hammer from the workbench and smashed the car window. He covered his nose with his arm, coughing on the black smoke, and yanked open the car door. Heat scorched his skin as he crawled into the back, but he wouldn't stop. Fearlessly he ripped down the split seat.

His heart swelled into his throat.

Cassie lay unconscious, bound and gagged.

With a strength Ryan hadn't known he possessed, he pulled her bloodied body out of the trunk and cradled her in his arms. Fire now fully engulfed the building. They had to get out of here and fast. He held Cassie close to his chest and ran. When they reached the garage door, a nearby shelf containing old fertilizers, paint thinners and bug killers exploded, throwing them out of the burning structure.

Ryan held his head, his ears ringing when he realized that Cassie lay sheltered underneath him. He rose to his knees, barely aware that backup had arrived in a blaze of flashing lights.

"Cassie!" He shook her.

No response.

He gently touched her bloodied and bruised head, panic gripping his heart. Ripping off her gag, Ryan tore open her coat and lowered his cheek to her nose, watching her chest for any movement. Tears mixed with soot as emergency personnel approached them. Single-minded in his task, Ryan couldn't hear what they were saying and batted them away with his hand. *Cassie, breathe, just breathe.* It felt like an eternity until her chest moved. Thank God.

"Someone get a medic!" Ryan yelled.

EIGHT

Leaning against the wall in the small hospital room, Ryan couldn't take his eyes off Cassie. The curtains were pulled, but the morning light came through, giving the room a soft, creamy glow. Above her left eye was a nasty gash that was swollen, with black stitches sticking out like garish eyelashes. Her bruising hadn't fully come in yet, but the promise bloomed across her right cheek in vibrant purple and yellow hues. Each mark upon her pale flesh a testament to how he'd failed her.

Doctor Helms had explained that Cassie was fortunate that she was only suffering from a bad concussion and minor lacerations. However, Ryan knew she was far more fortunate than the doctor understood. No one had ever survived The Wolf's capture. Cassie being found alive was a blessing, one he thanked God for and one he vowed not to take for granted.

He looked at her lying in the hospital bed.

Her eyes drifted shut during her questioning by US Marshal Sanderson.

This was the fourth time she'd been interrogated, the fourth time he had stood here listening to her answer the same type of questions. It could have been the hundredth time, and still, her words would bring visions of all the things The Wolf had done to her like it was the first. His jaw clenched as he tried to banish the images. This was all his fault. Why hadn't he been paying closer attention to her security?

Ryan glanced around the room, devoid of the usual cards and flowers. It seemed odd to see her in a space so empty of color and joy. He thought about her friends back home and how they would have been here in droves, supporting her with love and attention. How had he gotten everything so wrong about Cassie? And why hadn't he listened to Logan? Everyone else in Bakerton loved and trusted her for the good person she was, and he'd acted like a fool.

"You didn't mention that before." Marshal Sanderson's voice broke into his thoughts.

Cassie groaned, shifting down in her bed. "I'm trying my best."

"Then let's go over this again...from the top."

Ryan straightened. "The doctors said fifteen minutes, Sanderson. Time to back off."

"Who died and made you king of the hill? I have a few more questions," Sanderson said without taking his eyes off Cassie.

Ryan stepped away from the wall, his voice brooking no argument. "You've been hammering her with questions for over thirty minutes. She's done talking."

The agent shifted his weight on the wheeled stool and flipped back a few pages in his notes. "You said you left Agent MacIntosh's kitchen…"

Stalking forward, Ryan tore the marshal's notebook from his hands and lowered his face to within inches of the man. No one, marshal or not, was going to push Cassie beyond her limits. "She's tired, and I said she's done for the day."

Not one to back down, Sanderson rose slowly to his feet until the two men stood chest to chest, their eyes locked.

"Boys, that's enough," Cassie said.

Neither man moved. Eventually, Marshal Sanderson grabbed his coat from the hook on the wall. "I'll be talking to Agent Dunlack about this."

"Be my guest," Ryan said and took the man's seat without a backward glance. No one was going to hurt Cassie ever again.

"I'll be back in an hour." The hospital room door banged shut.

"Was that necessary?" Cassie asked, rubbing her temples.

"You tell me." Ryan rose and gently sat on the edge of her bed. His head tilted with concern. "Looks like your headache is back. Do you need the doctor?"

"No, I'm fine. It's just those questions."

"You don't have to answer any more of them if you don't want to," he said. "I can talk to Walter and..."

Cassie's hand rested on his, making his heart skip a beat. "It's not that. I want to answer the questions." She sighed. "It's just frustrating. I remember what happened, it's clear, and then I go to talk about it, and it's like grasping at memories through a fog. They take shape, and then everything becomes so muddled."

"Give yourself a break. You have a pretty nasty concussion."

"We don't have time for breaks," she snapped, and then immediately apologized.

"It's okay," he said, stopping himself from folding her into his arms. There was nothing he wanted more than to hold her close, but he wasn't her boyfriend. Not trusting himself, he moved off her bed and back onto the stool.

"Ryan, I—" She suddenly stiffened, her hand moving to the neckline of her hospital gown. "My clothes? Where are they?"

"They've been bagged for evidence. Is there something you wanted?"

Cassie met his eye with a look of distress. "I put some important photos in my jeans pocket."

"You've already given them to us."

"I did?"

Ryan rolled the stool closer and stroked her hair. "The concussion is affecting your memory," he said. "But, it's good that you grabbed those photos. Some of the women were still listed as missing." The sorrow that rose in her eyes made his chest squeeze tight. Ryan knew there were no words to ease what she was feeling, but he tried anyway. "There are families that will find closure because of you."

Cassie moved onto her back and stared at the ceiling, pulling away from his touch. "I can't stop thinking about those women. Some of them weren't even out of their twenties. I imagine their parents and how…" Cassie's voice cracked, and she shook her head as if unable to voice the thought. "Did you know that The Wolf calls them his loves?"

"His victims?"

"Yes. He believes it too. Fully believes that he loves them." Cassie shifted her head on the pillow, and her glassy eyes met his.

Ryan wasn't prepared for the naked vulnerability he saw on her face. He couldn't breathe. A rising need for vengeance tore through him like a howling wind. It took everything within Ryan to force that monster of emotion back into its cage. Cassie needed him here for her. He squeezed her hand, a lump rising in his throat. "We'll get him, Cassie. I promise you we're going to get him."

Rain pattered gently at the window while Cassie sat on the comfy chaise lounge in front of it, her mind a maze of thoughts. She looked up from her devotional, unable to focus on the words, and watched Ryan position kindling in the massive stone fireplace. Since coming here, to this safe house on the far outskirts of Willowridge, Oregon, she felt hyperaware of him. The way he always smelled of wood and leather, the sounds as he moved, the feel of his calloused hand on hers. These feelings made the disconnect between them all the more puzzling.

Ryan muttered under his breath, and he repositioned the wood in the hearth.

Internally, Cassie sighed. She had merely asked for a blanket, and there he was, making her a fire. If she so much as made a peep, he'd instantly be by her side. While the attention was sweet, it was getting to be a bit much.

The fire caught, and Ryan added some larger logs onto it.

The kettle began to whistle. "I'm making myself some tea. Do you want some?" Ryan asked, moving into the kitchen.

Her stomach twisted. They needed to talk, and this was her opening, but she didn't want to make things more awkward between them. Words from the pages she had just read flooded her mind: *For God hath not given us the spirit of fear; but of power, and of love, and of a sound mind. 2 Timothy 1:7.* She looked up and knew the prodding came from Him. *Point taken*, she silently prayed back and placed the leather-bound book on the coffee table.

Reluctantly, Cassie made her way over to the island, which also functioned as their table, and pulled out a stool.

"We need to talk."

He hesitated but didn't turn around. "About tea?"

"No. Yes. In a way."

Looking over his shoulder, he accidentally touched the side of the kettle, burning his hand. He flinched and began running it under cold water.

"You okay?" Cassie asked.

He gave a small smile that didn't reach his eyes. "Completely." He wiped his hands off on the tea towel and then filled a mug, placing it in front of her. "Are you hungry? There's not much here, just some stale crackers, but Kate will be back soon with groceries." He pulled open a tall cupboard and began poking around the pantry shelf.

"Please don't avoid this."

"I'm right here. What am I avoiding?" he asked, not turning around.

Cassie dropped her head into her hands. This wasn't going well. "You're not acting like yourself."

Closing the cupboard, Ryan turned and faced her, his brow furrowed with a hint of fire in his eye. "What do you mean?"

Her heart skittered. She knew that look all too well, but it was too late to back out now. "Well, it's just that you're being overly nice."

"You want me *not* to be nice to you?" he said coldly. "That's what you're asking?"

Her cheeks flushed. "No…sorry, I don't mean like that. I mean you're always getting me tea, making me a fire, grabbing my book. If I sneeze, you have a tissue…"

"So, I'm not allowed to make kind gestures toward you?"

"No, that's not it at all. It's just, whatever is happening here, this isn't us, and I want to go back to how things were."

Ryan grimaced. “Life doesn’t go backward. If it did, trust me, I’d go back to before I met you.”

A sucker punch directly to her gut would have been gentler. Cassie pushed away from the island and headed for the stairs. “Well, if that’s how you feel, then I’ll tell them I made a mistake and request a new security detail in the morning.”

“Cassie, wait,” he said, quickly reaching her side. “Let me finish.”

She kept walking, and he grabbed her arms, forcing her to face him.

“Let go of me.”

“I’m sorry,” he said, releasing her. “What I said came out wrong. Please, just let me explain. I’ve been thinking a lot about us the last few days.”

She stared up at the ceiling, blinking back her tears. There was no way she was going to let him see her cry.

“I always accused you of not telling me everything, but I realize now, I was just as guilty of holding back.”

“What?”

“I never told you why I left the FBI.”

“What has that got to do with anything?”

“That’s what I originally thought too, but now looking back on things, I think it’s got a whole lot to do with it." Ryan took a deep breath. "Being a federal agent, I was always dealing with the worst of the worst." His hand gently touched the bruise on her cheek and then fell to his side. "There was this string of bank robberies where the guy was rapidly escalating. We knew who was doing it, but we had nothing strong enough to make the charges stick." His jaw tightened. "My team got assigned to watch him, but he managed to slip through our net. He committed a robbery two days later where he shot and killed the teller, a single mom with a six-year-old boy."

"That's awful, but why are you telling me this?"

He looked her square in the eye. "Kate caught me planting evidence."

"No," Cassie said, stunned. There was no way the Ryan she knew would ever do something like that. "No. I don't believe it. Not you."

"Kate talked me out of it, and no one knows how close I came to crossing the line. It rattled me. I knew I needed a fresh start, so I moved back to Bakerton and I met you." A wry smile lit his face, and he took her hands in his. "I wasn't ready. I saw the world as this dark place, and you made me look at it differently. I was falling in love, and I panicked when I realized I didn't really know anything about you."

Cassie pulled away. "You know why."

"But I didn't then. I began thinking horrible thoughts about you, that you were using me for something. I knew I couldn't think clearly, and there were all these red flags around you."

"Ouch."

"I tried to cut you out of my life for the last year. I avoided your restaurant, switched churches, did everything I could to forget you. It didn't matter what I did. Every night before I closed my eyes, I felt the need to pray for you. Every morning I wondered what you were doing. The more I missed you, the angrier I was at myself. The more I tried to forget you, the more I'd find ways to catch sight of you. And now, now that I know the truth about your past, I'm so sorry. I'm sorry that I leaped to the worst conclusions. You didn't deserve that, but as much as I want to, I can't take back the past year. You were an amazing girlfriend, and I failed you. I continue to fail you, and sometimes I wish we had never met. Because if I had never met you, I wouldn't know what I had lost. I wouldn't worry about you like I do. I wouldn't..."

Her fingers came to his lips and stopped his words.

The front door opened, and Kate walked in, her arms loaded down with groceries. "Man, that store was a zoo," she said, dropping her keys on the entryway table. "I wasn't sure what to pick up, but I think I've got enough stuff." Her voice trailed off when Cassie quickly came to help her with the grocery bags, and Ryan turned away, resting a hand on the fireplace mantel.

"Looks wonderful, Kate," Cassie said, her voice a little too high in her own ears.

Kate didn't move from her stance at the door, her assessing eyes bobbing between Ryan and Cassie.

Staring at the crackling fire, Ryan cleared his throat. "I'm sure Cassie will be able to turn that into something incredible."

"I have to admit, I'm enjoying having a chef along," Kate said, with an undertone of suspicion. "Usually, these babysitting gigs have the worst food."

Cassie met Kate's eyes and turned away, not wanting to answer the questions that rested there. "I'll take that as a compliment."

With a whistle, Ryan signaled the dog to his side. "I'm going to walk the perimeter with Duke."

"Sounds good," Kate replied. "I'll give Cassie a hand in here."

At the offer, a hard knot formed high in Cassie's chest. Her whole world was reeling, and now she had to face down Kate in what was sure to be an interrogation. She pulled the groceries from their tall paper bags and began carefully inspecting the fruits and vegetables, doing everything to appear calm. "I'm thinking mashed potatoes, vegetable ratatouille and broiled salmon."

"Delicious."

Keeping her hands busy, Cassie set the veggies next to the sink. "Okay, then can you scrub up the potatoes and carrots?"

"I can."

Cassie pawed over the spices at the bottom of the bag, trying not to think of what might have happened if Kate hadn't walked in when she did. What else would Ryan have said? Was it merely her forgiveness that he was looking for? Kate turned on the water beside her.

"So, are you going to tell me what I just walked in on?"

"You didn't walk in on anything."

Kate found a regular rhythm with the potato peeler and smiled knowingly. "Oh yes, I did."

"There's nothing to tell." Cassie opened the lower cupboards, searching for pots and pans.

"Look, I'm honor bound to report if there is something romantic going on with you and Ryan."

Cassie kept her voice professional. "We're

friends. Nothing more." She found some pans at the far back of the cupboard and wrinkled her nose.

"That's what I thought," Kate said, scrubbing some carrots. "I mean, if you two were in a relationship, Ryan wouldn't be rejoining the FBI and moving to Portland."

What? Her heart dropped in her chest. *She's just trying to rattle you; don't let her.* Cassie stood up and placed her pans calmly on the counter. Stealing the water from Kate, she rinsed off a lemon and began cutting it into precise wedges. "He never mentioned that," she said.

"Walter has been talking to Ryan over the last year about rejoining the team, and it looks like he's finally accepted."

The words coming out of Kate's mouth erupted in Cassie's brain like tiny bombs. Was that what Ryan's speech had been about? Was he asking her forgiveness before leaving Bakerton, tying up loose ends? Cassie squeezed the lemon into a bowl, added some spices and began vigorously whisking it all together. The thought of Ryan moving bothered her, and she didn't like that it upset her as much as it did. If she were honest with herself, somewhere along this journey, she'd begun thinking that when The Wolf was caught, she would end up back in Bakerton. It scared her to realize how much she wanted Ryan there too. But according to Kate, he was moving on. Just like she needed to.

"His talents are wasted in a small town. It's a wonder he didn't get bored sooner," Kate said.

Bored? He found life in Bakerton boring? Cassie filleted the salmon with quick knife strokes and then brushed it briskly with her marinade. "It is a wonder," she muttered. With rough hands, Cassie encased the fish into a tinfoil package and placed it into the fridge.

"Can't wait to see him officially back with the nation's finest," Kate said, chopping the vegetables.

Cassie's fingers squeezed the door handle of the fridge. She had no reason to be angry. Ryan had every right to live his life as he pleased. She stared at her reflection in the stainless steel and took a deep breath. "When is the transition supposed to happen?"

"Not sure, but I don't think it'll be long. Ryan seemed eager to get out of that town."

Cassie felt sick to her stomach. "I've got the fish marinating, and you've got the veggies ready. Dinner looks like it's all prepped, and I'm exhausted. I think I'm going to go lie down for a bit."

"Okay, anything else I can do here?"

"Nope, you've done plenty."

* * *

Dinner had gone well, if not a little silently.

Ryan watched Cassie from the corner of his eye. She sat with her feet up on the couch, occasionally turning the pages of her book. It was a cozy scene, with Duke happily snuggled up close to her. From the way dinner had gone, he suspected if he approached Cassie, the temperature would instantly drop about forty degrees. He'd be lying if he said he wasn't confused by her frostiness. While their conversation earlier today hadn't gone as smoothly as he would have liked, it hadn't ended badly, or so he had thought. Ryan glanced at the clock. Thirty more minutes until Kate did her perimeter check, and he would be able to talk to Cassie privately. He wanted Cassie's forgiveness, and to at the very least, be friends.

"So, are you going to do anything with those letters over there or am I going to die of old age first?" Kate asked, drawing him back to their Scrabble game.

"Sorry." He sighed and gave his head a little shake. What he needed to do was get his mind back under control. Scanning his tiles, he spelled *axed* onto the board while Kate took a sip of her coffee. Her phone began vibrating and hopping across the kitchen island, banging against the Scrabble board and causing the tiles to rattle. Their eyes met, and his nerves lit up like a Christmas tree.

"MacIntosh. Yes. Copy that," she said formally to whoever was on the other end of the line.

Cassie pushed a disgruntled Duke off the couch and joined them at the island. "Everything okay?"

Kate raised her eyes to Ryan. He knew that look, and it didn't calm him. "Walter is on his way up," she said. He nodded, agreeing with what Kate wasn't saying. For the special agent in charge to come up here in person meant something was gravely wrong. Without hesitation, he took his position by the door, pulled back the blind and watched the headlights of Walter's car traverse up the hill. He took his gun from its holster and looked for any sign that something was amiss with the vehicle.

"What's going on?" Cassie asked.

"We're about to find out," Kate answered. "But for now, I'd like you to stay out of sight. Behind this corner, please," Kate said, gently shoving Cassie into the hallway.

Surprisingly, Cassie didn't argue, which told Ryan she was scared. He wished he could take that from her, but fear heightened the senses, and she just might need that. Walter parked his car in front of the house and plodded across the yard to the lit front porch. Nothing seemed suspicious, and yet Ryan remained on edge.

"Brrr," Walter said, coming in with a waft of cold air. "It's bitter out there." He unwound his scarf and set it on the hook by the door along with his coat.

Since it was clear there was no immediate danger, Kate and Cassie came out from behind the corner. With a grim smile, Walter motioned them all over to the couch. He sat in the wing-back chair adjacent to the fire and looked as drained as Ryan felt.

"Cassie, how are you doing?" Walter asked stiffly.

"Pretty good, all things considered."

"Glad to hear that. I apologize for my abrupt appearance. But there's been a couple of developments, one of which you need to be aware of."

Cassie looked to Ryan, and he took her hand in his, not caring what Walter or Kate thought about it. "All right," she said.

"The congressman's security agent, Gabriel Finch, was murdered in a prison fight three days ago."

A gasp escaped Cassie's lips, and she slid her hand out of Ryan's.

"Murdered," she repeated. "Was The Wolf behind it?"

"It's hard to say for sure." Walter shrugged. "Everything is pointing toward a beef Gabriel was having with an inmate, but we'll have to wait and see what the investigation turns up. At this point, we can't rule out that The Wolf got a prisoner to tie up a loose end on his behalf."

Cassie's eyes narrowed shrewdly. "What does this mean for me?"

"I need to discuss that with my agents. But for now, it is one less person that wants you dead."

Ryan coughed.

"Your agents and me," Cassie said. "If this is about the direction my life is going to take, I should have a voice in this conversation."

"Quite frankly, no," Walter said, putting up a hand to silence Cassie's further protest. "This is a federal investigation, and not everything is in your purview. Look, I've had a long drive, Cassie, and I need to speak with Kate and Ryan privately. I'm going to ask that you give us the room, please."

Cassie looked to Ryan, her eyes pleading for him to insist she stay, but he remained quiet. If Walter were a different person, his request for privacy would have been handled more diplomatically, but there was no helping that right now. As much as he disagreed with how Walter was handling this situation, this was work. This wasn't about Cassie's feelings. Cassie could be mad at him all she wanted, but he, Kate and Walter had a job to do.

Bristling from the dismissal, Cassie rose stiffly from beside him. "Fine," she said. "But I want it noted that Ryan does not make decisions for me."

Walter nodded.

When she reached the bottom of the stairs, Cassie paused. "Duke, come." With a jingle of dog tags, Duke found his place at her side.

Ryan sat still but could feel Cassie's eyes burning through him. He focused on Walter's polite smile as the man watched Cassie and Duke journey up the stairs. Walter waited until he heard the bedroom door click shut and then turned his attention fully onto Kate.

"What's going on?" she asked.

Walter leaned forward, his elbows resting on his knees.

"Look, there's no easy way to say this, so I'm just going to say it. Kate, this afternoon someone set fire to your home."

Her mouth dropped slightly open.

"Who? The Wolf?" Ryan asked, redirecting Walter's attention and giving Kate time to collect herself.

"We're awaiting final confirmation, but that's what we're thinking. The accelerant used at the Pine Springs cottage had a unique chemical makeup. Preliminary tests are showing it's the same accelerant used at Kate's house." Walter reached out and squeezed Kate's hand. "We didn't expect The Wolf would turn and target you and your home like this. I'm sorry. I really am."

"How bad is the damage?" she asked, shutting down his condolences.

"When firefighters arrived, your home was fully engulfed. There was nothing they could do to save it."

Her eyes closed briefly.

"If you want to go and see it for yourself, I can have another agent replace you here," Walter offered.

"No," Kate said, her voice lacking all emotion.

"Are you sure?"

"I am." She cleared her throat. "Investigators will have it sealed off. It's not like I can go in and sift through the damage. I assume you have a car watching it."

"I do," Walter confirmed and then drew his gaze back to Ryan. "I've reached out to Logan, and he has officers watching your home in Bakerton. The Wolf is rapidly escalating, and the two of you appear to have targets on your back."

Ryan steadied himself. "This changes the plan, doesn't it?"

"It does," Walter replied. "We were hoping that The Wolf would go underground until after Christmas, giving Cassie a few days to recoup, but that's not the case. He's on the warpath, so we have to assume an attack here could come at any time. I've ordered a small surveillance team to back you guys up, and they should be here shortly. But, Kate, if you need to tap out, now is the time. Are you good?"

A log crackled, then shifted in the fireplace.

Her eyes sparkled. "Trust me, I'm good."

NINE

The next morning, Cassie stood in the kitchen stirring her batter for gingerbread pancakes, trying to calm her racing thoughts. Maybe if one of the FBI agents had made chitchat, the atmosphere in the cabin would have lightened, but not one of them said a word. Not Kate. Not Walter. Nor any of the three new agents that had arrived earlier this morning.

Agents Thomas, Bell and O'Connor, the new arrivals, had brought with them an air of impending danger. While bright sunlight flooded the cabin, there was no more laughing, no calming smiles. Everything was about business. Even Cassie's wake-up call had been abrupt, with Walter pounding on her bedroom door and then spouting a curt debrief on their current situation. Apparently, the FBI team surveilling the cabin had found boot impressions in the woods and Ryan had gone out to compare them with the photos he'd taken of The Wolf's treads in

Bakerton. Maybe it was nothing—the tracks could be from a hiker or a hunter—but from the way everyone was waiting on Ryan's return, no one believed it was that simple.

Walter's phone rang.

"Dunlack," Walter said. He looked up from his seat at the island, meeting Cassie's eyes with a guarded expression. "You're sure? All right, then come back in."

Cassie's hand tightened on the wooden spoon, her breathing quickening in her chest. Was it good news or bad? She watched Walter tuck his phone into his pocket.

"Cassie," he said, waving her over. "Have a seat."

She set the bowl on the counter and wiped her fingers off on a tea towel. Part of her didn't want to move, wanted to refuse to hear what he was inevitably going to say. But that wouldn't change anything. They had all known it was only a matter of time before The Wolf found her. Now that the moment had arrived, there was no point in delaying it. Cassie moved obediently to the stool across from Walter.

"That was Ryan. He's confident that the boot tread matched the ones from the night you were stalked through the woods in Bakerton."

The news wasn't surprising, and yet Cassie's heart thundered all the same.

"I've already called in for a helicopter, and they're going to radio me when they are twenty minutes out."

"When they're twenty minutes out?" she parroted. A lot could happen in twenty minutes. "Can't we just drive out of here now?"

"We're in the middle of nowhere, Cassie. That has its perks and challenges. While it gave us an advantage in hiding you, the reality is, there's one road in and one road out. That right now is a big disadvantage. If we drive you out of here, The Wolf could easily ambush us." Walter rubbed the back of his neck. There was no mistaking the tiredness that ran through the line of his body, but the shrewdness that remained in his eyes made Cassie trust him. "The helicopter is your safest option. There's a clearing not too far from here where it can land. Agent MacIntosh figures it'll take you two about twenty minutes to hike to it."

"Just me and Kate?" she asked.

"Yes. The rest of the team will stay here. We know The Wolf is watching and bringing in a large security detail to escort you would be like painting a bull's-eye on your back, forcing him to attack. I think we can all agree we want to avoid that." Walter set a napkin onto the middle of the island. "Our team," he said, pointing to his side of the napkin, "will create a diversion out the front of the cabin using Agent O'Connor as your double." On Cassie's side of the napkin, Walter made two of his fingers tap like little running legs. "Meanwhile, you and Agent MacIntosh will escape out the back. It's a fairly simple plan, but I believe it'll be effective."

Just then, the cabin door opened and Ryan walked in, locking eyes with Walter. A silent communication passed between them. Then with a swift nod of Walter's head, he motioned all the agents into the sitting area for a strategy huddle.

Needing to keep busy, Cassie went back to making breakfast. She laid the bacon into a pan and prayed that her escape would go unnoticed by The Wolf. But what if it didn't?

She picked up the bowl of pancake batter and looked over her shoulder at Agent O'Connor. The woman was supposed to be her double, but Cassie didn't see how. They were both of similar build and height, but that was where the similarities ended. O'Connor had long, gorgeous blond hair, a sweetheart-shaped face with wide bow lips and small blue eyes. The woman's profile bore little to no resemblance to Cassie's oval one. While Walter had given O'Connor an auburn wig, it wouldn't be enough to fool The Wolf if he got close.

Ryan nudged her shoulder. "Don't you think you're overmixing those?"

Cassie looked down at her bowl and sighed. "Probably," she said and poured the batter into circles on the hot griddle, sending up a pleasing aroma. "O'Connor looks nothing like me."

"On such short notice, we're fortunate to have someone who even remotely resembles you."

"That doesn't inspire confidence."

Ryan sighed. "Trust me. This will work." He grabbed the fork from beside the skillet and turned the sizzling bacon. "The Wolf will determine she's you from a distance. With binoculars or a spotting scope, he's not going to have a clear enough visual to determine that O'Connor is a double. By the time he gets near enough to know for sure, the team will close in on him and it'll be over."

Cassie couldn't hide the skepticism in her eyes. Things were never that simple. "And you're staying here with her? You're not coming with Kate and me for the extraction?"

"The Wolf will expect me to stick close to you. If I stay here, it will help him to assume O'Connor is you."

Cassie flipped the pancakes. It made sense, but still. She didn't like it.

"That's part of why I came over," Ryan continued. "The chopper radioed. It'll be at the clearing in about twenty minutes. So you and Kate need to start hiking out."

Her heart clenched. "I don't like the thought of you staying behind," Cassie said, surprised her voice sounded as calm as it did.

"And I don't like being away from you," Ryan said, letting out a slow breath. He turned so that his hip touched the counter, and his gentle eyes met hers. "But it's the safest option right now." His hand started to move toward her shoulder, and then he quickly reversed the gesture, hooking his thumb into his pocket instead.

"I am sorry that I dragged you into all this." Her eyes met his. "If I could do it over—"

"Everything would have happened just the same." He smiled. "You forget. I didn't give you much of a choice about me coming along," he said, his voice soothing.

Cassie dropped her gaze to the pan, her hand lightly shaking when she used the spatula to put the pancakes onto a plate. His hand covered hers, and she stared at the sight, etching it into her mind.

"There's nowhere else I'd rather be," he said. "No matter what happens, you need to know that I would always choose to be on this road with you."

Cassie couldn't say anything over the lump in her throat.

"Now, Agent O'Connor is upstairs with a blond wig for you and a set of her clothes. Don't keep her waiting," Ryan said, taking the spatula and turning her toward the stairs.

It surprised Cassie how quickly and efficiently Walter's plan went into action. Disguised as Agent O'Connor, she had exited the back of the cabin with Kate like they were agents doing a perimeter check. So far, everything had gone smoothly. They hiked through the woods together with Cassie in front and Kate trailing behind, watching for signs of The Wolf. Even though it looked like their escape had gone unnoticed, it didn't stop Cassie from feeling skittish every time she heard Duke snap a twig in the bushes. The faithful dog roamed freely between her and Kate, often venturing into the woods before circling back to one of them. While Duke hadn't completed police dog training, he would bark if he noticed anyone out in the woods. Should Kate or Duke spot signs of The Wolf, Kate would let out a whistle, and Cassie was to run the trail toward the helicopter while Kate did her best to hold the assassin off.

When the path opened onto a broad rocky

riverbank, Cassie stopped short in the shade. Large cedar and hemlock trees dotted the far shore with distant rolling mountains that stretched for miles underneath the vast blue sky. If it had been under other circumstances, the sight would have mesmerized her. But these weren't normal circumstances, and the cold nip to the breeze made her feel overly alert.

She scanned the tree line and, seeing nothing suspicious, wandered out toward the water's edge. Cassie looked upstream, around a large boulder. Somewhere along here was a make-shift footbridge that would take them across the river and lead to the field. She closed her eyes. The thought of the chopper and the safety it offered brought mixed feelings. *Was Ryan safe?* There was no way to know for sure, and Kate, if she knew, wouldn't tell her until they were both secured on the helicopter.

Cassie turned her gaze to where the path exited the trees. Kate should be here by now. Her ears listened for any sounds from the woods but heard nothing over the burble of the river.

"Kate. Duke," she called, her voice shaky.

There was no answer.

"Duke!"

The dog bounded from the bushes, his eyes sparkling with excitement.

"Where's Kate, Duke?" she asked quietly, her heart beating faster. Cassie pulled a leash from her pocket and bent down when a large rock exploded into tiny pieces behind her. She dropped to the ground, her ears blazing from the high piercing scream as another bullet careened past her. Duke bolted for the bushes. Another rock splintered into pieces, sending hot shards across Cassie's back. She needed to get to cover. Cassie moved her hands from her ears and kept low, scrambling up the bank to the trees.

Where was Kate?

Cassie darted into the woods, heedless of the branches that scratched at her arms and slapped her face. She dared a look over her shoulder when a bullet zinged past her hip, skinning the bark off a nearby tree. Pushing herself harder, Cassie leaped over decaying logs and struggled through the brush that caught at her feet. Fear accelerated her pace, but the shooter's footsteps crashed through the forest, not far behind her. *Run*, her brain screamed. Her throat burned, her lungs pumped, but no matter how hard she ran, his footsteps continued to gain on her. *Run faster.* But still, he was closing in.

Arms circled her waist as a body knocked her to the ground in a somersaulting tackle. He grabbed onto her ankles and pulled her toward him, snapping her chin hard on a gnarled tree root. Frantic, Cassie grabbed onto a low tree limb and tried to drag herself free, but his rough hands held her secure. Desperate to escape, she lashed out with her legs.

A vice-like grip flipped her onto her back. Cassie squinted up at The Wolf, the bright sun blinding her eyes. He sat proudly on top of her, towering like one of the tall trees behind him, his heavy weight holding her hostage.

"You're mine," he said, reaching forward to subdue her hands.

"Never," Cassie growled, managing to snatch a hand free. Quickly, she raked the ground until she felt a rock the size of her palm. Grabbing it, she slammed it hard into his nose and heard a splintering crunch over his scream of pain. Warm blood erupted over both of them. She rocked her hips and threw him off, then scrambled to her feet and bolted into the forest.

Like a rabbit from a fox, Cassie ran without direction, her thoughts focused solely on escape. She burst into a small clearing of cedars and hemlocks. Her lungs screamed for breath and Cassie stopped running, gasping in large, painful gulps of air. The sunshine filtered through the trees in long beams of light, and all she wanted to do was drop to the ground from exhaustion. Her legs were turning to rubber, making her realize she couldn't keep on as she had been.

The forest stood utterly silent.

Where was she? Could she find her way back to the cabin? Water. She could hear the jostling river below her. Jogging up a short, forested rise, she crossed a small expanse and stood at a rocky ledge. Maybe she could follow the river back and find the footbridge to the helicopter on the other side.

"Cassie," came his nasally call. "Come out, come out wherever you are."

Her heart pulsed. There was no way she was going to outrun him. *Hide.*

Crouching low, she slid under the heavy fallen boughs of a hemlock tree and sidled up to the trunk.

"Cassssssssssie." This time his voice was closer. "I don't like playing games." His feet thudded methodically up the rise.

She shifted closer to the trunk, pulling her knees up to her chest, and drew her head down into a ball. Her traitorous breath came in short, ragged gasps. To her own ears, it sounded like a beacon calling out to him. Through a small opening in the branches, she could see him standing with his back toward her in the exact spot where she had stood just moments ago.

"You're foolish if you think you can hide from me." He turned, facing her now. His muted brown tuque had a soft brim that shaded his eyes, but she felt the anger in them.

She curled up tighter, her chest pumping hard against her arms. *Keep calm. He's lying. He doesn't see you. Block him out.* Silently, she began to pray.

"Just come out from under there."

She closed her eyes tighter.

"I was with the army, Cassie, and you leave tracks like a moose." A hand grabbed the collar of her shirt and roughly pulled her through the scratchy screen of branches. "If only you had been a good girl. Things could have been different," he said, looking down at her. "Stand up and turn around."

Cassie rose to her feet as defiance swelled in her chest. Standing tall, she looked him directly in the eye, refusing to budge.

"Turn around," he said, drawing his handgun.

She said nothing, just stared at him.

He sighed and shook his head. "If this is the way you want it, so be it. Freedom has marked its time. You. Shall. Be. Set. Free."

He raised his gun. Her mind raced, but there was no way to escape.

Cassie closed her eyes.

The tree limbs rustled, and Duke launched himself through the air. He caught hold of The Wolf's arm, sending the assassin into a tailspin. Ryan burst up onto the rise just as The Wolf squeezed the trigger, firing aimlessly. Duke fell with a hard thump but quickly got up and positioned himself in front of Cassie, snarling protectively. The Wolf raised his gun, training it on her. She didn't dare move.

"Drop your weapon. Drop it now," The Wolf yelled at Ryan.

Ryan took a cautious step backward, drawing The Wolf's complete focus.

This was her chance. Gathering her courage, Cassie moved just like Gerald had taught her, and roundhouse kicked the gun from The Wolf's hand. The Wolf expertly twisted, and as he was about to strike, another gunshot pierced the air. The Wolf dropped to the ground in front of her.

Cassie stood still, unable to move at the sight of The Wolf's body lying motionless before her. With his weapon drawn, Ryan kicked The Wolf's gun farther away, sending it scuttling across the ground.

"Cassie!" Ryan called.

Her pulse drummed frantically in her ears. She looked up and realized Ryan was by her side, talking to her, but her mind wouldn't register his words. Her limbs felt numb and refused to move. She stared down at them, puzzled. Ryan touched her shoulder, grabbing her attention. Again, he repeated words to her, and she had to think about them, about what each word meant. Suddenly what he was saying made sense, and she sat down on a large mossy boulder, her breathing jagged, her limbs shaking.

She stared at Ryan, watched him reach into his coat and don a pair of crime scene gloves. Systematically, he began searching The Wolf's pockets, disarming him as he went.

"Is he dead?" she whispered.

Ryan's shoulders drooped. "Yep."

Cassie squeezed her eyes shut, afraid to ask her next question. "Where's Kate?"

He didn't say anything.

Cassie opened her eyes. He was still crouched over The Wolf's body, his face wearing a solemn expression. *Oh, dear God, please no.* "Ryan." Her voice cracked. "What happened to Kate?"

He cleared his throat. "Kate was knifed and left tied to a tree."

"Knifed." The single word seared through her heart.

Ryan completed his search of The Wolf's body and sat down on a nearby log, looking exhausted. Duke lay at his feet. "He meant for her to bleed out. But I got to her in time. She's going to be okay. A medical team is being choppered in."

Relief flowed through her.

"And Duke?"

He stroked the dog's back. "He's completely fine. Aren't you, little buddy?"

The river lapped noisily, filling the silence. It all seemed surreal. It was over. It was finally over, and they had all survived.

Emotions began to swirl with memory, fear mixed with relief, laughter with sadness. It all felt so hard to comprehend. Cassie stepped over The Wolf's gun and found her place by Ryan and Duke's side.

Ryan clamped his arm around her. Fiercely, pulling her close, he kissed the top of her head. His warmth soothed her soul. All she wanted to do was close her eyes, to soak up this feeling and pray that it would never end. In his arms, the world felt right. Tears choked in her throat when she attempted to force them back. She was about to fall apart, but this wasn't the moment for that. A team of agents would be descending on them soon.

She swiped at her eyes. "How did you know we were in trouble?" she asked, keeping her eyes from The Wolf's body.

"Kate missed her check-in. She never misses her check-in. She's like clockwork when it comes to stuff like that." He looked over at The Wolf and kissed her head again, then let her go.

Cassie nodded. "I just can't believe it's over."

"We don't know that yet."

"What do you mean?"

A scowl etched Ryan's face. He stood and moved to the small pile of things he had removed from The Wolf's body. He held up a phone. "There are messages on this, but I can't read them."

"Is it encrypted?"

His brow furrowed. "No, it's not like that. It's more like a code," he said, swiping through some screens. "The texts are times followed by a message written in Wingdings."

Cassie paused. "Bring it here, let me see that..." He squatted beside her and shifted the phone, letting her examine the messages. She couldn't believe what her eyes were seeing. All of a sudden, everything made sense—the assassination, her being hunted, everything. She inhaled deeply. "Did you find anything else on him?"

"A few weapons."

"Anything else, anything odd?"

"A bookmark."

She doubled over. This was bad; this was very bad.

She didn't want to ask, but she had to. "The bookmark, does it have a modern art motif with a bunch of circles on it?"

Ryan looked at her quizzically. "Yes."

"Show me."

"What's going on?" Ryan asked.

Cassie felt like she was going to be sick. "I know who contracted the hit on Congressman Johnson."

"What are you talking about?"

"I made that bookmark, and what's more important is that there's an identical painting to it."

"Why is that important?" Ryan asked, his eyes narrowing in puzzlement. "What has any of this got to do with Congressman Johnson?"

"It's got everything to do with him." Her throat felt thick, making the words she had to speak stick. "A former client of mine, Elaine Baccara, commissioned that work. Within the art on that bookmark, I've hidden the key to deciphering the code on The Wolf's phone."

TEN

There should have been FBI agents and US marshals swarming all over the cabin, in the yard and down by the river. Instead, Cassie sat tucked under Ryan's arm on the porch swing by the cabin's back door, listening to the creak of the chain as they swayed back and forth. In some ways, the worst was behind them. The helicopter had left hours ago, taking Kate to the hospital. Her surgeries had gone well and—thank the Lord—a full recovery was expected. That news had led them here to the porch swing, its rhythmic movement soothing in a jangled world that neither of them wanted to think of. Her head snuggled into Ryan, and all she wanted to do was absorb every detail of this moment. For a wisp of time, they were safe. She let the sun warm her face, listening to the distant call of birds, and deeply inhaled the scent of the forest.

She slipped her hand into Ryan's, feeling

his gaze drop to hers. Her fingers longed to reach up and touch his stubbled jaw, but she let them stay where they were. Believing she was about to die had made her realize truths that had gotten hidden under the muck and mire of their complicated relationship. She cared for Ryan. She knew that now and accepted it for what it was. She also understood, beyond any doubt, that he would do anything to keep her safe. This last year, things had become awful between them. They had barely been on speaking terms, and the actions that had transpired were hurtful, but that was the past. There were words that still needed to be said, but nothing changed the core truth. She forgave him for everything.

Across the field, the trees rustled with movement. Walter pushed past a young pine tree and stopped short at the sight of them together.

His sudden appearance made Ryan's arm instinctively tighten around Cassie while his foot slowed the swing. Their break from the chaos was over.

Shaking his head, Walter didn't wait to see if they'd follow, just charged past them into the cabin.

Not letting go of Cassie's hand, Ryan squeezed it.

Whatever happened, in the next few moments, they would face it together. For the first time in a long time, she knew that she wasn't alone.

Walter stood at the kitchen counter, pouring himself a cup of coffee. The late afternoon light streamed in through the window behind him. "Explain it to me again," he said briskly.

Cassie sank into her chair at the wooden island. "We've gone over this."

His spoon clinked harshly against the ceramic mug as he added two large dollops of powdered creamer. "I have lost count of how many protocols and procedures I have broken today. Not only that, but you're accusing a prominent businesswoman, who has more high-powered political friends than you can imagine, of having a United States congressman killed, and that's after the FBI cleared her of any wrongdoing!" He swirled his coffee with rough strokes and sat across from her. "It's my career that blows up if you're wrong. Explain it to me again."

Annoyed by the dance Walter was playing, Cassie's voice came out tight. "Nothing has changed from our last three conversations with you."

He eyed her stonily, raising a brow at her tone.

"I'm sorry," she said. "If you just give me

five minutes with that bookmark, I can decode The Wolf's phone texts and prove to you that I'm right."

Walter took the spoon from his coffee and carefully laid it on a paper napkin.

They all knew his real dilemma wasn't granting Cassie access to the bookmark. The real problem was the answer to a tough question: Did Walter *want* to know that Cassie was right? At this point, he could still pull back and stick his head in the sand, suppress the truth and retire unremarkably in the next three years. However, once those messages became deciphered, Walter would be tossed into a wonderland maze that none of them could turn back from. With retirement so close and the risk of losing everything so high, Cassie didn't blame Walter for his hesitation, but she prayed he would make the right choice.

"Come on, Walter," Ryan said.

Walter released a guttural groan and looked at them both. "The technicians are on their way in, but I have to respect the chain of custody. I don't want that bookmark getting tossed out of court. It has to be handled properly."

"I promise. I won't even take it out of the evidence baggie, and the crime scene technician can stand over my shoulder the whole time I have it."

He took a tight sip of his coffee. “Fine, but you listen to the tech, and you do everything he says.”

Anticipation hummed within her. “Thank you, Walter. You won’t regret this.”

“Let’s hope not,” he said and began talking into his radio.

Within minutes, Agent Miguel Garcia, a close friend of Walter’s from the FBI’s evidence response team, came in with the bagged bookmark. Carefully, he draped the island with a white cloth and placed the bookmark on top. Miguel then laid out for Cassie a clipboard with two crisp sheets of paper, a pencil and a few other tools that he quickly showed her how to use.

This was it. Reaching for the bag, her arm trilled with nerves. She wasn’t sure what the message would reveal, but she hoped it would be incriminating enough to put Elaine behind bars for a long time.

Walter stood up from the island and stepped back to the kitchen counter. He took a final sip of his coffee and set it in the sink. When he turned around, the three of them were all staring at him.

He shrugged his shoulders. “Let’s get to it, shall we?”

Ryan and Miguel leaned close on either side

of Cassie while Walter reassumed his seat across from her. *No pressure*, she thought, taking a calming breath.

She placed the bookmark under the wide-field magnifier and, just like she knew they would be, found the hidden symbols. Seeing them eased the tension in her shoulders. Art was what she knew and holding something she had created felt like meeting an old friend.

"Did you make this?" Ryan asked, his tone impressed as he put his hand on the back of her chair.

"I did," she replied, meeting his gaze. It felt good to share this intimate part of herself with him, despite the circumstances. Art was intrinsic to who she was. It revealed a part of herself that, until now, Cassie had been forbidden to share with him. "Yes. As I mentioned before, this bookmark is a miniature of a work that Elaine Baccara commissioned." Cassie took a sheet of paper and drew a large circle on it. "This bookmark, like the larger piece it is based on, has a hidden cipher in it that cracks a complicated code that Elaine created."

Walter cleared his throat. "Cassie, I've studied the dossier the Marshals compiled on you, and this picture wasn't in it."

"It wouldn't be. Elaine had me sign a nondisclosure agreement, so the public has never seen this drawing. Under the NDA, I am forbidden to discuss the existence of this work or reveal any of its secrets."

"But since it was used in the commissioning of a crime, your NDA is void," Ryan said.

"Exactly."

Along the edge of the large circle Cassie had just drawn, she drew twenty-four smaller circles, laid out like positions on a clock, equally spaced. Looking through the magnifier, she quickly transposed the random letters she saw on the bookmark into the small circles she'd created. All three men leaned in closer to understand better what she was doing.

"The movement of color in this piece," Cassie began, "inspired me to create a series of works that have three connected scenes with circles superimposed, binding the parts together." Cassie took a long pair of tweezers and began pointing out the details. "In this piece, I used the circle to bind various illustrations of power, intellect and love."

Walter nodded, looking at her with newfound appreciation.

"But this piece is far different from any of my other works." Cassie drew another circle, a smaller version of the larger one, but she began filling in symbols this time instead of letters. "I created this piece with pen and ink to allow for the intricate design, which I did using high-powered magnifying glasses." Cassie finished plotting the symbols for the smaller wheel and then cut out the two circles.

"Why would anybody go to all this trouble when phones are so well encrypted these days?" Ryan asked.

Not looking up from her task, Cassie explained, "Elaine runs PyrceTech, the computer-security company responsible for maintaining computer firewalls, upgrading software and operating IT support for government offices. Including the FBI." Cassie paused. This next part was a little unnerving, considering everything that was going on. "She told me that smartphones could be decrypted easier than the government wanted the public to believe. Remember World War II and how the Allies had broken the Enigma code, but they didn't want the Germans to know?"

Ryan nodded.

"It's much the same with modern-day cell phones. The government wants people to trust the encryption so that criminals think their messages are secure when in reality, they're not. Elaine told me that old-school codes with pen and paper could be more secure when done in the right way. Since I was creating the work of art, she had to explain her code to me and how it worked."

Cassie placed the small circle she had just made inside the larger one, her pulse racing. This was it—the first solid clue binding Elaine to The Wolf. Her hand slightly shook as she aligned the wheels, like inset dials on a safe, into their starting positions. Cassie looked at the time transmitted before the code and then began moving the circles accordingly. Instantly, she began jotting down letters, and letters started forming words.

TEN LADUKE RD WILLOWRIDGE

Cassie moved the dials again.

IMPATIENT FOR PROOF OF

Her heartbeat quickened as the letters formed the next set of words.

CASSANDRAS DEATH BEFORE CHRISTMAS.

Cassie looked up and made eye contact with Agent Dunlack. His voice sounded grave, like he hadn't spoken in years. "Well, that's an awful Christmas present." His words hung heavily in the room. "So let me get this right.

You think this message came from Elaine Baccara, head of PyrceTech." He paused. "That she sifted through our computers, discovered that we had you here and gave The Wolf this address."

"I believe so, yes."

Walter's head nodded absently. "So PyrceTech, the company I call when my computer goes down, is run by the person who hired The Wolf to kill you and most likely Congressman Johnson." Walter closed his eyes and breathed deeply, his nostrils flaring. "The woman, whose company is embedded in our FBI computers like a weed, has orchestrated one of the most notable assassinations in US history."

"It looks that way." Cassie's eye's drifted over the words she had just written, their intent sending goose bumps over her flesh.

How many hours had she spent studying cryptology in hopes of impressing Elaine? Her cheeks flushed red with the memory of how happy she had been to take that woman down into her private studio and show off her work. She had all but begged Elaine for the commission. Cassie leaned back in her chair, trying to push down her anger. All the schmoozing had been unnecessary. Elaine was nothing if not calculating. She would have chosen her to be the artist before ever setting foot in the gallery.

Cassie laid down her pencil. Because of one woman, she had lost everything: her family, her identity, her career. Everything. And why? Because Elaine had decided it should be so.

"Not just our computers," Miguel said, putting away his equipment. "PyrceTech recently assumed the contract for several other government agencies. They now look after the IT support for the US Marshals' computers as well."

Ryan put his hand on Cassie's shoulder, but she could barely feel it. She couldn't feel anything. Her thoughts began twisting like thorns in her mind.

"I don't understand this. Elaine and her company were thoroughly vetted by the world's top agents when they were bidding for the government contract," Ryan said. "And they passed a second rigorous investigation after the assassination of Congressman Johnson. The investigators should have found something."

"You'd think," Walter said softly, "but it makes sense. Congressman Johnson was a House Intelligence Committee member and sat on the subcommittee reviewing the privatization of IT maintenance. Johnson was a very vocal opponent, and Elaine faced a lot of scrutiny because of that, but she and her company still came out clean." Walter pushed his stool back from the island. "I don't know how our teams could have missed this," he said, his tone laced with irritation.

Neither did Cassie, but if anyone was capable, it was Elaine. The woman was brilliant, and nothing proved that more than how close she had come to pulling off the high-level assassination and still coming out on top. A tremor ran down Cassie's spine. "It explains how The Wolf tracked this safe house and all the other locations we've been."

"And why Elaine has never stopped hunting you." Ryan sat heavily in the chair beside her. "Your knowledge of the code links Elaine to both The Wolf and the murders, making you a dangerous loose end."

"At least now, with The Wolf's phone and the code, you've got the proof. You can arrest her," Cassie said, hopefully.

"It's all circumstantial," Walter said. "Criminals at The Wolf's level change out burner phones about twenty-five times a year, so his texts will only go back a few weeks. It's unlikely that anything we find on that cell will link him and Elaine to the congressman's death." His brow furrowed. "Technically, we can't even prove who sent that coded message. We have good reason to believe that it was Elaine, but any decent lawyer would tear that apart in court." Walter fixed his gaze on

Ryan and then let it flicker over to Cassie. "But we do have an advantage here. Elaine doesn't know that The Wolf is dead. We could make Elaine believe that he's captured Cassie for his own devices again."

"Walter—" Ryan shook his head "—that's too risky, and you know it."

"I'm not asking for Cassie to be directly involved," Walter said, his eyes narrowing thoughtfully. "We'd use Agent O'Connor. I believe she is still out in the woods documenting the scene." Miguel nodded, and Walter continued, "What we need is for Elaine's hands to get dirty. Otherwise, a scapegoat is going to take the fall for all of this. For us to catch her, we need to entice her with something she wants more than anything. And what she wants more than anything is Cassie." Walter tapped his index finger on the table. "Let's get Agent O'Connor in here and work out a game plan."

Cassie frowned. *Agent O'Connor?* That trick hadn't fooled The Wolf, and as far as she was concerned, it wasn't going to fool Elaine either. The only thing it would accomplish would be tipping that woman off and sending her on the run. The thought of Elaine getting away with everything riled Cassie. That woman needed to be held accountable for all that she had done.

"What can I do to help?" Cassie asked.

"At this point," Walter said, rubbing his eyes, "nothing."

Nothing? He couldn't be serious. Cassie stared at Walter in disbelief. "You need me. O'Connor didn't fool The Wolf, and she's not going to fool Elaine. She'll figure out The Wolf is dead soon enough. Don't squander this advantage." Cassie's gaze bobbed between Walter and Ryan. Their faces set in hard lines already told her their answer, but still, she pushed to be involved. "Elaine's in the government databases. Who knows what she's doing with all that information she's mining. You can't risk things going sideways because O'Connor doesn't look enough like me. I want to be of service. I can do this."

Walter picked up the evidence bag containing the bookmark and studied it with his naked eye. "We appreciate all that you have done for this investigation, Cassie, but I think it's time you go sit in the living room while we figure the rest of this out."

Her cheeks flamed with indignation. She opened her mouth to argue when Walter leaned back in his chair, his arms crossing over his chest, daring her to say something. Her eyes narrowed to slits. There was no point in uttering a word. Not one of the three men at the island was going to listen to her concerns.

They had gotten what they wanted from her, and now she was to sit nicely and pretend the dismissal didn't sting. But it did. Elaine had destroyed her life, and now Cassie was supposed to sit idly by. With her chin held high, she stood and made her way to the couch, her thoughts rolling like thunderclouds.

While Cassie had always known she was being hunted, for the first time, she knew who was behind it. Her life, the one she had lived as Cassandra Roberts, had been stolen by a person she'd once considered a friend. The bitter betrayal lit a slow-burning fuse within Cassie.

Elaine Baccara, she repeated slowly to herself, *is impatient for my death.*

She sank into the soft cushions of the couch, her fury making the memories from the alley eight years ago come sharply to life. Like it was yesterday, she could smell the musty stairwell. Hear the clicking sound of the town car door shutting. Feel the way her heart pounded when The Wolf had emerged from the car. See The Wolf's hand reaching into his pocket, pulling out the glistening wire and brutally garroting the congressman. Her memories rolled on, the dialogue between the congressman's security agent and The Wolf playing back to her like an old movie.

Not the plan, The Wolf had said. *Where's the girl?*

She got sick. Left, his accomplice had replied.

Cassie's chest felt tighter and tighter, the words scorching into her mind.

For years she hadn't thought much of that conversation. But now, each time her mind replayed it, it became clearer. She was *the girl.* Cassie closed her eyes, and visions of Elaine in her black silk gown, advancing through the crowded gala, flared vividly before her. What would have happened that night if she had talked to Elaine instead of letting Sylvia handle it? Cassie's heart smoldered bright with anger. Elainc would have maneuvered her into the back alley with the congressman. All these years, Cassie had believed she was accidentally caught up in this nightmare, but there was nothing accidental about any of it.

From the moment they had met, Elaine's intentions had been for her to die the night of the gala.

Ryan sat cautiously beside her on the couch, jolting Cassie out of her thoughts. She could tell from the look on his face he was debating how to defuse the situation. But really, Cassie thought, what could he say? Walter was his boss, and she knew Ryan agreed with his decision to exclude her. She bit the inside corner of her lip, stifling the words that wanted to pour out.

"Walter could have handled that conversation better," Ryan said.

Sarcastically, Cassie raised an eyebrow. "You think?"

"I do," he said earnestly, "and I'm sorry."

"But you don't disagree with him."

"You're a civilian, not an agent. That's the bottom line. Our job is to make sure you stay protected and safe."

Civilian. The word rankled her nose. She was a civilian. She couldn't argue with that, but Cassie wanted to point out that she had been an incredibly useful civilian. And what had that gotten her now that the investigation was heating up? Now that she wanted to see Elaine pay for what she had done. Inside, Cassie was seething, but it wouldn't do any good for Ryan to see that. She lowered her eyes, desperate for control over her emotions.

His fingers fell gently on her wrist. "Kate is lying in a hospital, and you're still black and blue. I want Elaine behind bars more than *anything*, but not at the expense of your life."

Cassie's jaw tightened. There was nothing she could say to that, and they both knew it.

"I understand that you guys don't want me

involved, but it doesn't change the facts. Whatever you're planning with O'Connor isn't going to work." Venom broke into Cassie's words. "Me acting as bait is our best shot at *ending* this."

Ryan sat back as if she'd punched him. "There's a lot of hatred in your tone."

"Are you kidding me right now?" Cassie's eyes narrowed. "You know what she's done, the people she's hurt, the people she's killed. I want justice."

"Do you?" Ryan asked, tilting his head slightly. "Because it's a very fragile line between justice and vengeance."

"I don't need a lecture," she said, turning toward the coffee table. Wasn't he a fine one to talk? Hadn't he just shot The Wolf? He had no problem delivering justice then.

"I know because I've walked it. Once you cross the line, it's hard to come back." Ryan pulled out his worn leather wallet from his pocket and plopped it on the couch beside her. She watched him remove a plastic three-by-two-inch scripture encouragement card from inside. Reverently, Ryan stared at the faded plastic. "You know how messed up things were between my dad and me." His voice lowered while his fingers toyed with the edges of the card. "I hated him, Cassie. I'm not proud of it, but I hated that man for everything he had done to me."

"You put him in jail."

"I had a part in it, yes."

"It felt amazing to put him there, didn't it? Be honest."

He frowned while he contemplated his next words. "My need to catch him nearly destroyed me. Putting my dad in jail didn't right the horrible things he'd done." Ryan paused. "About a week before we caught him, there was this cop who'd been after my dad for a long time, a Detective Marsden, who did something that I didn't understand at the time."

"What was that?"

"He gave me this." Ryan handed her the card.

She flipped it over and read it out loud. "'Micah 6:8: He hath shewed thee, O man, what is good; and what doth the Lord require of thee, but to do justly, and to love mercy, and to walk humbly with thy God?'"

A hollowness spread in Cassie's chest. She didn't want to hear this.

"Marsden told me that his father had this card made for him when he joined the force. His old man had said it was something worth remembering. It was a gutsy move, Marsden giving it to me. I could have had him written up for it." Ryan let out a breath. "Anyways, he did, and I've held on to it all this time. I'd like to say I understood the message right away, but I didn't. My dad went to jail, and it felt incredible for a while, but it didn't stop the anger. So I joined the FBI, I started hunting other bad guys, and when I caught them, there was this high. For a time, I would feel better. But then it would end, and I'd chase after the next criminal with an intensity I couldn't explain. When I reached the point of planting evidence, I started reading that card more and more, and over time it became a North Star for me. Pointing me the right way when I was going off track."

"Ryan, stop."

"Just think about what that verse means."

Cassie held the card out for him to take it back.

"Keep it for me. It's important," he said, gently pushing her arm back toward herself. "I'm worried about you and who this is turning you into."

Cassie stared down at the card clutched in her hand. "Elaine deserves to be behind bars."

"I'm not saying that she doesn't. I'm not saying that my dad didn't. What I am saying is acting justly, loving mercy and walking humbly is a balancing act. When one of those three principles is weighted wrong, we stumble. I care about who you are, don't let Elaine change that. Guard your heart and be careful."

Walter called over to Ryan. "Hey, enough lollygagging. We've got a plan we have to work out."

ELEVEN

Cassie looked at the code Walter had asked her to send to Elaine on behalf of The Wolf. It was a simple message, but she double-checked her work to ensure she hadn't made an error. The Wolf was a lot of things, but he was not sloppy. The fire popped loudly in the fireplace of the cabin, sending a shiver down her spine.

JOB COMPLETE. MEET IN
PERSON FOR PROOF OF
EXECUTION. AWAITING MEET LOCATION.

"I'm ready to send," Cassie said, and Walter gave her the official nod. It did not feel satisfying to send the text. Nor did it feel pleasing when Elaine took the bait and responded twenty minutes later with a location in Northern California.

Through the planning process, it was decided that Agent Thomas would impersonate The Wolf while Agent O'Connor played dead in the trunk. In Cassie's gut, she knew the scheme was not going to work. Regardless, the small protective team from the cabin would go in advance to the meeting and set up the perfect sting. But Cassie didn't trust it, not that anyone listened to her.

The only agents not going with the advance team were Ryan, Miguel and Agent Bell. Walter had decided to split the men between two tasks. Ryan and Miguel were to drive back to Portland with the evidence to ensure it was kept secure. Meanwhile, Agent Bell would take her to a safe house on the northern coast of Oregon. Every step of the operation had been thought out, and all concerns neatly tied up.

Still, something ate at Cassie's stomach. Ryan had been polite and listened to her, but having *a feeling* that something was wrong didn't hold a lot of weight with the law enforcement side of him. Nor, when she really thought about it, should it. Still, the misgivings had a deep hold on her gut, and now that Agent Bell was telling her it was time to leave, every part of her screamed not to.

Cassie stood on the front porch and took one last look through the front window at Ryan. He stood chatting with Miguel in the living room with his back toward her. It was time.

She let out a slow breath and tried not to think about what she was doing. Turning her back to the scene, Cassie slung her duffel bag over her shoulder and began walking toward Agent Bell's black Crown Vic.

With the fall of darkness, a sharp cold had settled over the mountain, but Cassie couldn't feel it. She couldn't feel anything. While the agents inside were hopeful about their strategy, Cassie's mind had already followed the trail of what would happen when Walter's plan failed. And fail it would. Whether the FBI realized it or not, Cassie knew she was in the process of closing off one life to start another. Her hand gripped the handle of her bag tighter. She would not look back at the cabin.

In the past, when WITSEC had forced her to relocate, Cassie had always found something to be hopeful about. This time there was nothing. A sad smile spread across her lips. How could there be? This time she knew who she was up against.

Elaine was Teflon, and like Teflon, she would skillfully avoid Walter's trap. Then, for the rest of her life, Cassie would be on the run with hit man after hit man coming after her. There would be no happily-ever-afters in Bakerton. No Ryan. She bit her lower lip, forcing back the crushing grief that surged. Why had she ever allowed herself to hope that things might work out between them?

She lifted her face to the wind, letting nature cool her rising emotions. Not only was she to lose everything again, but this time it wouldn't be The Wolf hiding in the shadows. It would be an unknown assassin, one she wouldn't recognize. The next person assigned to kill her could be anyone: her taxi driver, her waiter, the person jogging by her on the sidewalk.

Light snow fell softly on Cassie's coat collar, and she stared up into the starry sky.

"Cassie, wait!" Ryan yelled from the front porch of the cabin.

She turned to see him, the light from the cabin outlining his form. He grabbed his coat from the hook by the door and came to her side. Even in the dark, she could tell he was smiling down at her.

"Were you just going to leave?"

Cassie blinked back the tears that wanted to spill down her cheeks. The smile on Ryan's face told her that he didn't see the permanence of this goodbye. He didn't get it. Despite everything she had said to him, he didn't see that the writing was on the wall. She was going to be on the run for the rest of her life, and she would never see him again. "How do we say goodbye?" She met his eyes. "Because I don't know how to say those words to you."

His gaze dropped to her lips. "This isn't forever. You'll go with Agent Bell—"

"And then what?"

"The team will catch Elaine, and you'll come back to Bakerton."

His optimistic words burned through her heart, bringing bitter tears to her eyes. This wasn't fair. None of it was fair. She turned away from him, pressing the heels of her palms to her eyes. "Ryan," she said, anger at the situation spilling into her voice. "You won't be there, so what does it matter?"

"What are you talking about? Why would you say that?"

She whipped around to face him, the fury feeling so much safer to handle than the sadness. "Kate. Kate told me that you were rejoining the FBI. That means Portland, doesn't it? Isn't that where the field office is?"

Ryan rocked back on his heels, the surprise of her words evident on his face. "It's complicated."

"Isn't it always?" she said, letting out a huff of breath. "We're really good at complicated."

He smiled at that.

"Look," Cassie said, "I'm off to protective custody, off to northern Oregon, and you..."

She let the words trail off, harnessing the emotion within. "…and you're off to Portland. We both know the future is not in our control."

The falling snow dusted Ryan's hair and the shoulders of his coat in white. The distance between them, while mere steps, felt like miles. Cassie longed for the situation to be different, but no amount of dreaming would change reality.

"I can talk to Walter," he said. "I'm sure we can work something out." Ryan's warm hand cupped her cheek, drawing her eyes up to his. "*We'll* figure something out. I know we will." So easily, he moved through her defenses, making her want what could not be. He leaned down toward her, and despite herself, Cassie's heart raced. She began to rise on her tiptoes when movement in the cabin doorway caught her attention, and she saw Walter step out onto the porch. Cassie pulled out of the embrace, using her sleeve to swipe at her watery eyes. "You've got to go."

His hands gently pulled her closer. "This isn't going to be forever," he said, looking deep into her eyes.

"Can you promise me that?" she asked, her voice wobbly.

"No."

"Ryan," Walter called. "We need you inside."

A trite smile flashed across Cassie's face. "Walter is waiting," she said and tried to pull out of Ryan's grip.

But Ryan didn't move. Instead, his hands slipped down to hers and held them tight. "We're going to catch Elaine, and I'll figure out something with Walter."

"Have you met your boss? He doesn't seem like the 'we'll make things work' type. And even if he was, let's face it, my future isn't that simple. With everything we've discovered, it doesn't matter whether I'm in WITSEC or with the FBI. It's all going to end in the same result. They're going to force me to relocate and change my identity." Cassie stared up at the sky and then met his tender blue eyes, her heart aching. "So whether we like it or not, our future is decided."

"Cassie—"

"Agent Matherson. Inside. Now."

Unable to put off his boss any longer, Ryan let his hands fall from hers and began walking backward toward Walter. "I don't believe this will be forever," he said.

She watched him go until he disappeared back inside the cabin. "I know," she whispered under her breath. "I know you don't."

Agent Bell came up next to Cassie's shoulder. "Ryan's a good man," he said. She looked up at the lanky FBI agent who, until now, had never spoken to her directly. From what she had seen of him, he was a quiet man who kept mostly to himself, but his face was kind, and that put her at ease.

"He is," she said, exhaling.

"You ready to go?"

Cassie stared at the cabin one last time. "Yep."

Agent Bell opened the rear car door for her, and she sat inside, careful not to look back. There was only a life of running now, and who knew where that was going to take her. The car journeyed down the hill, the snow turning into rain that splatted hard on the windshield. Part of her wanted to believe that she would see Ryan again, that she was wrong, but the arguments of her heart could not convince her mind. Tired and broken, Cassie let herself drift off into prayer, thankful that Agent Bell didn't expect a lot of conversation on the drive.

By the time they reached the interstate, Cassie stared sightlessly out the window, the steady whoosh of traffic and taillights acting like an anesthetic to her aching heart. Cassie wasn't sure how much time had passed when she noticed Agent Bell signal to leave the I-5 at the city of Eugene.

"Where are we going?" she asked.

He smiled at her in the rearview mirror. "I just need to make a quick stop," he said.

Ryan leaned back in the passenger seat of the Ford Explorer while Miguel drove. His mind was a maze of thoughts. When his cell phone rang, he didn't look at the caller ID, just picked it up. "Matherson," he said, expecting it to be Walter.

"Is that any way to answer a phone?" the prim female voice said. "It leaves me most undecided as to what I should call you. Officer Matherson? Or Agent Matherson? Your status seems to be changing by the minute these days, and it's hard to keep up."

"Who is this?"

There was a derisive laugh on the other end of the line. "Oh, Ryan. You must be more intelligent than that. Of course, you know who this is. And if you're smart like I think you are, you'll do your best not to alert Agent Garcia as to whom you're speaking with."

Ryan had never heard Elaine's voice before, and yet he had no doubt that was who was on the other end of the line. "What do you want?" Ryan said, his voice tight. If Elaine was phoning him, it not only meant that the sting had failed, but there was something she wanted from him. His hand squeezed the hard plastic of the phone. And that meant she had something to leverage. His chest filled with dread.

"To the point. I appreciate that." She let out a sigh. "It seems that you and Agent Garcia are transporting some evidence that I would like to be in possession of."

"Why would I help you with that?"

"In Troutdale, did you ever wonder how The Wolf slipped past Agent Bell, a highly trained FBI agent?" Elaine paused, letting the thought sink in. "It's odd, don't you think? Agent Bell watched the rear perimeter and didn't notice a man carrying a drugged woman down to the river?"

Under his breath, so that Miguel wouldn't hear, Ryan said, "Kate would only work with agents she trusted. I don't believe you."

"Bureaucracy is my friend, Ryan. Every move the FBI makes requires reams of paperwork. It's rather tedious for someone like you, but all that organized information is a treasure trove for me. For example, finding which agents were assigned to Cassandra Roberts's protective detail in Troutdale took—" Elaine exhaled contemplatively, then continued "—mere keystrokes."

Ryan squeezed his eyes shut. This couldn't be happening.

"Once I knew Agents Thomas and Bell were

tasked with the job, how long do you think it took me to turn one of them?"

"You're just spouting words. They mean nothing."

"Check your phone, Ryan," was all Elaine said before hanging up.

Immediately his phone dinged, alerting him that he had a text. Ryan steeled his stomach and prepared himself for the worst. It was a casual picture of Cassie in the back of Agent Bell's car. From the angle of the photo, it was apparent that whoever had taken that picture was sitting in the driver's seat. Whether it was Agent Bell or not, Elaine had someone very close to Cassie.

Ryan rubbed his knuckles pensively over his lips. How many men were on Elaine's payroll? If she had gotten to Agent Bell, then it called into question everyone on the team.

"Who was on the phone?" Miguel asked.

A smile spread across his face. *You'll do your best not to alert Agent Garcia as to whom you're speaking with.* There's only one good reason Elaine wouldn't want him to do that. Miguel was not on her payroll.

Cassie turned her head toward the passenger window. Agent Bell's explanation for taking her picture felt off. No decent agent would take a photo of a client in protective custody. Her identity, right down to the features of her face, was a heavily guarded secret—after all, her very life depended on anonymity. She stared into the stark fluorescent brightness of the gas station parking lot, hoping to see another motorist, but there was no one around. A growing sense of alarm snaked down her spine.

"I need to go inside," Agent Bell said, motioning to the station. "Sit tight."

She nodded, keeping her gaze focused out the window, afraid that he could sense her apprehension.

Agent Bell stood outside the vehicle and leaned on the open door. "You want anything?"

"No, thank you," she said, making her voice sound cheery.

"Suit yourself then," he said, closing the door and walking around the side of the painted white brick building.

Cassie ripped open the zipper to her duffel, instantly noticing that her gun case was gone. Frantically, she rifled through the bag, her heart thumping in her chest. Her cell was missing too. "No, no, no," she mumbled to herself. The FBI team must have gone through her things and confiscated anything they felt was threatening. She slammed her fist into the seat beside her. What was she supposed to do now? Something wasn't right about this scenario, and whatever it was, she wasn't going to stick around and find out.

With her bag in one hand, Cassie slid across the leather seat. Already she suspected the door wouldn't open, but she pushed on it anyway, praying that she was wrong. The door didn't even wiggle. She squeezed her eyelids shut, helplessness welling in her chest. Agent Bell could be back any minute. She couldn't give in to these emotions.

Cassie scanned the inside of the vehicle, looking for anything she could use to defend herself, but the car was immaculate, with not even a coin in the cup holders. She peered out the window for any sign of Agent Bell's return. While Cassie didn't know his habits, she doubted there was much time left. She yanked open her duffel again. There had to be something of use in here—shirts, cash, pants, toiletry bag. Toiletry bag. She held her breath, hoping whichever FBI agent had gone through her things earlier hadn't been a zealot. Cassie unsnapped the roll of toiletries. Her fingers traced over the items, settling on a pair of nail scissors. They weren't much of a weapon, but they were better than nothing. She tucked them into the arm of her coat and prayed.

* * *

It had only been an hour since Elaine had called, and still, Ryan hoped that he had made the right choice in looping in Miguel and Walter. His finger tapped the plastic folding table. Maybe he should have gone rogue like Elaine wanted. He pushed the thought from his mind, not for the first time. Waiting in this construction trailer was pushing him to the brink. It was an awful place that both looked and felt like a sauna. He tugged at the collar of his shirt and stared at Agent Maria Anand, the IT specialist Walter had brought in, who sat calmly typing beside him.

"Would you like some water?" he asked.

Her eyes lifted for mere seconds from their computer screen before returning to their task. "No."

He stared at the door. What was taking Walter and Miguel so long, and why had he agreed to wait here while they secured all the needed equipment? He sighed. He knew the answer. They had contacts with the other agencies that remained uninfected with Elaine's software, and he did not. His fingers tapped a fast beat on the table, making Maria stop typing and look at him. He smiled sheepishly and folded his hands together.

Waiting was awful.

Would their two-part plan work? Calling Elaine for information on the exchange—the evidence for Cassie—while Maria secretly recorded the conversation was the easy part. Part two—the actual trade and getting Cassie back safely—was what made his stomach bubble with nausea. *What could go wrong?* he thought sarcastically.

The metal door swung open, and Walter bustled into the room with Miguel in tow. Walter handed Maria a burner phone and sat next to Ryan. Unable to hold back his questions, Ryan asked, "Is there any new information on Agents Thomas or Bell?"

"We have Agent Thomas under surveillance, and so far, we've seen nothing suspicious."

"And Agent Bell?" That was what he really wanted to know.

"We can't tip our hand. If I check for the GPS location of his vehicle, Elaine is going to know immediately. Under normal circumstances, I wouldn't search for that information. I cannot look for him until he misses a check-in. You know this."

"So you haven't heard anything from him since he left?"

"He's not due to call for another two hours."

Ryan smacked the table harder than he intended. "Cassie could be anywhere in two hours."

"Pull it together," Walter said. "Elaine has no reason to hurt Cassie so long as she believes a trade for the evidence is possible."

He did know it, but it didn't mean he liked it. Ryan stood up and moved to the window, saying a prayer under his breath. Cassie's life was in God's hands, and he needed to remember that.

"We're about ready to get started," Walter said calmly. "Everything is in place. Are you going to be able to do this?"

Ryan took a deep breath. "Of course," he said and returned to the table.

"Okay," Maria said, placing the new phone on the table in front of Ryan. "It's ready to go. Walter," she said, excitement gleaming in her eye, "this recording software you got from the ATF is amazing to work with. We need to get something like this at the FBI."

Ryan looked at her then down at the burner phone. To her, this was just another case with cool new toys, but it was so much more to him.

Walter touched his shoulder. "This is going to work."

After a few keystrokes, Maria looked over at the men. "I'm ready on my end."

Walter nodded to Ryan.

This was it. Ryan blinked back the emotion he was feeling. What he needed to do was concentrate on the task at hand—a phone call. There was nothing more simple than that. He dialed in the numbers left on his caller ID from when Elaine had phoned the last time.

"Hello," came the clipped, professional voice.

Ryan waited a moment. "Hello, Elaine," he said, keeping his voice even. "This is Ryan Matherson. I have the evidence you requested, and I'm willing to exchange it for Cassie."

"An intriguing proposition, but you understand that I require assurances."

"What kind of assurances?"

"Text me a picture of the bookmark and cell on top of today's newspaper with the date showing. That will be the first step."

"And what kind of assurances do I receive that you haven't hurt or harmed Cassie?"

"None."

Ryan shook his head. "That's not how this is going to work."

"Yes, it is."

"Do you want the evidence or not?"

Elaine laughed. "Let's be clear. The state you receive Cassie in depends entirely upon you. Do as you are told and little harm will come to her. Misbehave and, well, there will be consequences."

"I could put the evidence back."

"And risk Cassie being hurt? I don't think so. No, Ryan, in this scenario, I am the one calling the shots. The FBI knows the evidence is gone, and from the reports coming in, you're the one they're looking for. Your career is over. Your freedom is in jeopardy. The only positive thing that can happen for you is Cassie's release. You'll follow my rules."

She had him, and they all knew it. "I'll send the photo within the half hour. What then?"

"Once the photo is received, I'll send you details about the exchange."

TWELVE

Agent Bell sat in the driver's seat, his brown eyes flickering up to the rearview mirror. Cassie flashed him a smile.

"I need to use the washroom," she said, gesturing toward the small building behind the gas station.

The agent sighed with annoyance. "You'll need a key from the store. Just make it quick, okay?" He got back out of the car and briskly opened her door, letting in a gust of fresh wet air.

Freedom was so close that she could almost touch it. Cassie slid across the seat and stood with her duffel in hand. She turned to say that she would only be a minute when she saw Agent Bell's eyes narrow on her bag. Instantly, she realized her mistake, but it was too late.

"What do you need that for?" he asked, gripping her shoulder.

Cassie lashed out with the tiny scissors, stabbing the back of his hand. Agent Bell cried out, reflexively letting her go. She sprinted across the slick parking lot, past the closed restaurant and minimarket doors, scanning for where to go next. A white compact car drove down the service road toward her. Desperate, she waved her hands over her head and dashed toward it. The car slowed down, and relief washed over her as she approached.

"FBI, get down on the ground."

Cassie looked behind her to see Agent Bell in his FBI jacket chasing after her with his gun drawn. The motorist, seeing the agent signal him on, stepped on the gas and took off without a backward glance. Her heart plummeted in her chest. She did not doubt that Agent Bell meant to kill her. Her only hope was to run. She dodged past the gas station's large propane tank and bolted down the road.

Ahead of her, Cassie saw a chain-link fence that secured a service yard for a soda pop company. Semitrailers sat parked in methodical rows, providing multiple avenues for her to escape. Pumping her arms, Cassie ran as hard as she could, expecting at any moment to feel a bullet tearing through her back.

Terrified, she threw herself at the fence. Her fingers gripped the chain-link, and just as she was about to start climbing, rough hands grabbed her shoulders and tossed her to the ground. Landing on her stomach, Cassie lay gasping for breath. Without mercy, Agent Bell wrenched one arm behind her back and then the other, locking her wrists in handcuffs and hauling her to her feet.

"Back to the car," he said, shoving the muzzle of his gun between her shoulder blades.

Agent Bell pushed Cassie onto a dining room chair. She grunted at the indignity, her arms sandwiched behind her—what she wouldn't give to stretch them out. They ached miserably from being cuffed behind her while they traveled in the car. Cassie wriggled in the chair, knocking her ankle against one of its legs. He hadn't tied them.

"Where are we?" she croaked, aiming to keep his attention on her face, not her feet. Agent Bell said nothing. Instead, he wandered to the door and looked down the hallway.

Even though he didn't answer, she had her suspicions. They'd entered through the rear gate of the estate, but Cassie hadn't missed the exquisite landscaping or the massive size of the home. The dining room, where she was now seated, was long and decorated in various textures and shades of reds and whites for Christmas. At the end of the room, heavy satin drapes stood open, revealing a stunning view of the ocean. There was little doubt in Cassie's mind that she was in one of Elaine's residences. The woman had often talked of her designer homes that she held scattered around the world.

As if on cue, Elaine strode into the room with a stout military-looking man beside her. "Sam. Take Agent Bell to my office," she said, keeping her eyes on Cassie. When Sam reached the door, she called to him again. "And Sam, have someone dispose of the car we provided Agent Bell in Eugene. I want no evidence that they were ever here."

Sam nodded and disappeared down the hall with Agent Bell.

Elaine, dressed in tailored business attire despite it being the wee hours of the morning, stepped to the edge of the sliding glass wall system. She stood for a moment in the moonlight, then swiftly closed the drapes before turning on the lights.

Cassie scowled. "The FBI, the Marshals, they'll come after me."

"Eventually," Elaine said. "But for now, everyone who's aware you're missing is highly motivated to suppress that fact."

A chill spread through Cassie. Elaine was right. None of the agencies charged with watching over her would realize she was gone until she didn't reach the safe house. It would be hours until that information came to light.

Elaine moved to the tall buffet and poured herself a cup of tea. "I'd offer you some—" she shrugged "—but your hands."

"You could uncuff me."

"I could, but that would create more excitement than I would like at this early hour." Elaine carried her white teacup and saucer to the beech wood table and sat across from Cassie.

The pungent scent of green tea made Cassie's empty stomach turn, but she kept her face blank while her mind raced. Why on earth was she having tea with Elaine? By rights, Agent Bell should have killed her long before now. Cassie's breath caught—unless Elaine needed her for something.

"Don't look so glum," Elaine said. "Everything will be over soon enough."

"For one of us."

Elaine's smile broadened, her cockiness getting under Cassie's skin. Well, if the woman wanted to play games, she had a few tricks of her own to play.

"You know, I never thought it was you." Cassie glared. "If I hadn't gone down into my studio that night, you would have had me killed with the congressman. That was your plan, wasn't it?"

Elaine shrugged. "As they say—two birds, one stone."

"Why? Because I knew about the code in the painting?"

"That and the congressman was an admirer of your work," Elaine said. "Your aversion to politicians made it impossible for him to obtain a private meeting with you. It was the one thing I could offer that he couldn't resist." Elaine sipped her tea. "Your gala was the perfect lure. Everything was arranged. If you hadn't disappeared when you did, I would have talked you into getting in that town car with him."

"I wouldn't have gone."

Elaine's eyes shone with amusement. "You forget how desperate you were to impress me."

Cassie's hands clenched into fists. The truth in Elaine's barb stung like a nettle.

"It was all arranged. The Wolf would have transported you both to a hotel room where he was to stage it to appear like a murder-suicide. Had you just followed the plan, everything would have been much simpler."

"Sorry that my feeling unwell got in your way," Cassie said caustically. "Why didn't you reschedule?"

"There was a strict timeline that couldn't be altered. So we made do."

"Made do? You rushed, and because of that,

I witnessed the assassination and became a dangerous liability."

"I'd say more of an inconvenience."

"One that must be of some use. Otherwise, I'd be dead right now."

Elaine tipped her head. "There is some evidence that I'd like in my possession, and in exchange for your safe return, Ryan seems more than happy to bring that to me."

"He would never do that."

"Wouldn't he?" Elaine's eyes twinkled. "You underestimate how much he cares for you."

Cassie stared down at the table. She shook her head, a sickening feeling rising in her gut. Would he cross the line to save her life? No, Cassie thought resolutely. No, Ryan would never do that. But Elaine's words began sprouting thoughts of doubt. Ryan had also come close to planting evidence once. If he did do what Elaine wanted, not only would he lose the job he loved but his freedom as well. Bile burned the back of her throat.

"You'd force him to ruin his life and not even think twice about it," Cassie said. "And all for what? Money? Power?"

Elaine carefully set her teacup on its saucer. "What Ryan chooses to do or not to do is ultimately up to him."

Cassie strained against her handcuffs—visualizing her hands around Elaine's neck. "I won't let you use me against him." She stood before Elaine could react and ran from the room, bursting into the hallway.

Sam, walking toward the dining room, stopped, stunned by Cassie's appearance. He raised his gun, but the delay gave Cassie just enough time to duck behind a column before he fired.

"Don't shoot her," Elaine called, entering the hallway. "We need her alive."

Cassie looked around her and saw the front door. She made a dash for it, but Sam's feet were swift behind her. He tackled her to the ground. With everything she had, Cassie fought, biting and kicking.

"Hold her still," Elaine barked.

Sam pivoted and straightened his body, pinning Cassie flat to the floor. His heavy weight pressed the air out of her lungs, forcing Cassie to lay helpless as Elaine walked toward her.

"Did you really think it was going to be that easy?" Elaine said, gripping Cassie's arm and stabbing it with a syringe.

"We need to go in there," Ryan said from his seat in the back of the surveillance van, only to have Walter shake his head no. He looked over at Maria for support, but she sat engrossed in her computer with Duke sleeping on a cushion by her feet.

Seated across from Ryan in the poorly lit van, Walter spoke patiently. "SWAT isn't here yet. You need to wait."

"But that was a gunshot."

"We don't know that for sure, and your meeting with Elaine isn't until 4:00 a.m., which—" Walter looked at his watch "—is an hour away."

"So Cassie is supposed to sit tight until then?" Ryan's head fell back against the van wall. Walter was unbelievable.

"We don't know what that sound was, and it's doubtful Elaine would kill Cassie before the exchange. She needs her alive for the time being."

"Walter..."

"What are you going to do? You need backup, and SWAT is thirty minutes out. You can't saunter up to the front door an hour early and rush the exchange," Walter said, his voice brimming with anger. "That kind of stupidness could get both you and Cassie killed. We wait for SWAT to arrive."

Ryan clenched his fists. He shouldn't be challenging his boss like this, but Cassie's life was on the line. "We all know what gunfire sounds like. She could be hurt. We have an obligation to Cassie's well-being."

"And I have an obligation to yours," Walter said vehemently. "Two dead is worse than one."

The words punched the air from Ryan's chest. Cassie dead. He shook his head. He couldn't think like that. "I can find a way to get in unnoticed," Ryan said, determined.

"Really, Houdini? We have no idea where the security cameras are situated. We don't know how many guards there are. You'd be going in completely blind."

"Not completely blind," Maria piped up from her computer station. "I've been partially able to hack into Elaine's security system. I've gotten access to the schematic showing the exterior camera locations. I just haven't broken into their video feed yet." Duke stretched his front paws, and Maria reached down to ruffle his fur.

"How long will it take to get the video?" Walter asked.

"I'm working on it, but Elaine's system is intense," Maria said, keeping her eyes on her monitor. "Ryan, look at this." She pulled the screen on its bracket away from the wall and tilted it so Walter and Ryan could see better. "If you cross the fence here, next to the rhododendrons, you should be able to cross the grounds to the house undetected."

Ryan turned to Walter. "Elaine's scrambling. She's not had time to prepare for any of this properly. Let me check on Cassie. Like you said, the SWAT team is on its way. If Cassie's hurt, me going in now could save her life."

"What happens if you get caught?" Walter asked.

"It's not the worst thing. Elaine knows I'll come after Cassie, and it's believable that I'd try to rescue her without handing over the evidence. It gives me an opportunity to get Elaine talking. If I get captured, it won't blow the operation."

Walter grumbled.

"Cassie's not a trained agent. My going in improves her chances of surviving this."

With a loud exhale, Walter fixed him with a pensive stare. "You won't be able to wear an earpiece. If they catch you, they'll check for that." Walter reached into a drawer and pulled out a cross pendant necklace. "You'll only have this. It's a one-way listening device—we'll be able to record and hear everything you hear, but we will have no way of communicating with you."

"I can handle this."

"Fine, but go quickly, and if she's okay, you get out of there unseen. You hear me?"

The main house was extraordinary, with its soaring black paned windows and off-white brick walls. Tall cedar topiaries decorated with white lights and Christmas ribbons flanked the stairs leading up to two massive front doors. But being the uninvited guest that he was, Ryan was careful to keep to the shadows.

Going around the side of the house and down the slope, Ryan made his way to the back of the mansion. The home had been built into the cliff and boasted a palatial walkout basement. Ryan couldn't help but shake his head when he saw all those windows. Windows that inflated his risk of being caught. He kept low, carefully moving off the wet grass and onto the flagstone patio, positioning himself behind the outdoor kitchen. From this vantage point, he could easily analyze the two-story estate before him.

The bottom floor of the house remained dark, with no movement. However, the second floor boasted several rooms that glowed from behind their drapes. A curtain swayed, and a bright flash of light cut into the night as a door slid open onto the covered balcony. Ryan crouched lower. A stocky figure emerged and leaned on the rail while he lit a cigarette and took a deep puff. Ryan could hear Elaine say something but couldn't make out her words from this distance. The man quickly stubbed out his cigarette and went back inside, but the door didn't completely close behind him.

Ryan stared at the open doorway above him. Risky, but potentially a good entrance point. He scurried across the patio to a basement window and tried it. Locked. Not surprising. He looked at the brick wall that led up to the covered balcony. His fingers were going to take a punishing, but there was no helping it.

Soundlessly, Ryan scaled the wall and pulled himself up over the rail. He stretched flat against the house, his ears tuned to the slightest of sounds. Carefully, Ryan stalked toward the open door, his heart thundering. The closer he got to Cassie, the harder he found it to keep his mind on task.

"It's not like she's going anywhere," said a gruff male voice.

"Nathan," Elaine said, "I don't know where Sam got you from, but if you don't act like the professional I hired, you won't live long enough to regret it."

"Yes, ma'am," Nathan said as Elaine's heels clicked an angry retreat across the hardwood floor.

Cautiously, Ryan pulled back the drape. Nathan stood with his back toward him. The man, built like a heavyweight boxer, would not be easy to take out. Shifting position, Nathan moved, and Cassie suddenly came into view. Ryan's heart lurched. She sat in a chair on the far side of the dining room table, with her head hanging forward and a gag in her mouth. She was so still.

Nathan rubbed the back of his neck. His eyes casually scanned the room and drifted over Ryan's location, suddenly widening.

Instantly, Ryan launched himself into the room. Years of training turned into reflex as the two men fought with ruthless skill. Thrown backward across the table, Ryan grabbed a heavy candlestick from the centerpiece and struck Nathan, rendering him unconscious.

His chest heaved. He looked over and saw Cassie raise her head. Swiftly, he moved to her side and pulled the gag from her mouth. She smiled a crooked smile. The sight filled him with more than just relief.

"Ryan?" she said drowsily.

"I'm here."

"She drugged me." The words came out slow, and her eyes struggled to stay open. "I don't like her."

Ryan caressed her cheek, thankful she was alive. More than anything, he wanted to kiss her. "I know, sweetheart. We'll get her."

Cassie's head tilted to the side, and she looked at him thoughtfully. "You called me sweetheart?"

"I did, but we need to get you out of here. Do you think you can stand?"

"Yep," Cassie said but didn't move a muscle. "I'm standing."

Ryan ran his fingers through his hair. They definitely weren't leaving the way he had come in. "We can do this together. I'm going to put my arm around you, okay? On the count of three, we're going to stand."

Managing to get Cassie onto her feet, Ryan took her to the doorway. He leaned forward and peered around the corner. The front door stood partially open, and he could hear muffled voices coming from its direction. They didn't have much time.

Gently, he squeezed Cassie's hand. "You're going to need to be really quiet. Can you do that?"

Cassie moved her finger up toward her lips but missed and hit her nose. "Shhh," she said.

"Exactly," he replied, his pulse racing. Pulling them forward around the corner, past the kitchen, Ryan prayed for a staircase, but instead, he saw a carved mahogany door at the end of the long hallway.

"So tired," Cassie whispered, her weight starting to lean more heavily onto his shoulder.

"Hang in there, okay? You can do this. We just have to make it to the end of the hall." Or so he hoped.

Behind them, Ryan heard the front door

close, and a male began talking with Elaine. Ryan's pulse pounded. "Just a little faster," he said, urging Cassie into a quicker pace. But the faster he tried to move, the slower her steps came. "You can't stop now," Ryan begged, almost dragging her forward.

He could hear Elaine's voice echo down the hall. "You're sure, Sam? I will not tolerate another misstep," she said.

"I'm confident," Sam replied. "Everything is exactly as you've requested. I'll load up the girl, and this will all be over soon."

"Not soon enough for my tastes," Elaine said.

Ryan pressed his eyes shut. It wouldn't be long now until they discovered that Cassie was gone. He stared down the open hallway before them, trying not to panic. There was no cover anywhere. If they got caught here, they'd be sitting ducks.

Cassie stumbled, her feet catching with his. They staggered a couple of off-balance steps before falling onto their hands and knees. Ryan kept still, holding his breath and listening intently for any hint that Elaine and her men were on their way. But there was nothing.

"I think I'll just take a little nap," Cassie said, moving to lie down on the floor beside him.

Ryan gripped her shoulders. "Hey, hey, hey.

We can't do that yet," he whispered. "Cassie, look at me." Her eyes opened. Her pupils were abnormally large and dark as she tried to focus on him. "Stay with me."

Cassie smiled.

"On your feet." He draped her arm over his shoulders and held her tight around the waist, hoisting them both up. Ryan looked behind them. There was no sign of Elaine or Sam yet, but time was ticking. They could discover Nathan unconscious on the dining room floor and Cassie missing any second now. He squeezed her hand. "I just need you to walk with me until the end of the hall, okay?" Cassie nodded and focused on her steps until they fell into rhythm with his.

"You smell really good," she slurred and inhaled deeply. "I really like that about you."

Ryan tenderly shushed her. "Just a little bit farther."

"That and your eyes. I think your eyes are so dreamy." Cassie's head lolled against his shoulder. "If only you weren't moving away."

They reached the doorway, and Ryan shifted her weight. His hand paused for a second over the door handle while he sent up a silent prayer that it wasn't locked. "Cassie," he said, opening the door, "you really need to be quiet."

"Shhh," she said again.

"Exactly."

Together they stepped inside Elaine's home office and closed the door. Ryan turned, and stopped, stunned. Hanging on the wall behind an oak trestle desk was Cassie's painting that he'd seen in miniature on The Wolf's bookmark. Nothing could have prepared him for the mesmerizing impact of seeing the real thing.

"So sleepy," Cassie said suddenly, and went limp in his arms.

"Cassie." Ryan tapped her cheek, laying her on the ground. Her breathing was slow and shallow, but it was there. He blinked with relief. But how was he going to get her out of here? Staring across the office, he spied a glass door that led back out onto the covered balcony where he had come up. There was no way he could get her over the railing and safely down now.

"Find her!" he heard Elaine yell.

A flare of panic spiked through Ryan. He scanned the room and spotted a pocket door. Quietly, he slid it open to reveal a short corridor with two more doors. Running straight ahead, he opened the one at the end. A small powder room with not enough space to hide in. Closing it, he slid open the last door—a storage room. Good enough. Carefully, he picked Cassie up and carried her inside.

The small, L-shaped room held wall-to-wall bookshelves containing rows of boxes and binders. *Where to hide?* Ryan moved about the room when his eye caught a knee wall–attic access panel. He said a prayer, wrapped his fingers around the frame of the panel and pulled. It screeched, making him wince. The cavern was larger than he'd hoped for, easily hiding the two of them. Filled with hope, Ryan picked Cassie up, tucked her inside and climbed in after her. Taking ahold of the access panel, he tried to maneuver it back into place, but the wood had swelled over the years and refused to close.

Ryan's mind raced. He hated to leave her but leaving the panel ajar would only act like a flashing sign, advertising their hiding spot. He needed to lure Elaine's men away. Ryan looked at his watch. Roughly fifteen minutes until SWAT arrived.

He lifted his necklace up to his lips. "Walter, Elaine's drugged Cassie and she's completely incapacitated. I can't safely get her out, with the chase being this close." Ryan pressed his eyes shut, knowing what he had to do and the risk he would have to take. "The only play I have is to keep Elaine's men distracted and away from Cassie until SWAT gets here." He was telling Walter where he had hidden her when he heard footsteps in the hall. "They're almost here." Ryan's heart thudded.

Leaving the space, Ryan fit the access panel back in as best as he could without making a ton of noise. It was almost flush, but a sharp eye would notice it. He spotted a neat stack of white Bankers Boxes and pushed them over, obscuring the attic access just enough that someone might miss it.

A creak from the hallway startled him.

Ryan slid behind the door, his breath feeling trapped in his chest. It was an awful hiding spot, but he flattened himself as best as he could against the wall.

The light in the corridor clicked on.

Slowly, the door swung open, lightly tapping Ryan's chest. Sam stalked by him in a low lethal stance, the weapon in his hand sweeping the room. Ryan waited for the security agent to turn the corner. When he disappeared from sight, he grabbed the door handle and slammed it shut, hoping to draw Sam into a chase and away from Cassie.

Bursting through the office, Ryan moved out the glass door and onto the covered balcony. Halfway across the deck, a reflection appeared in the window before him. Sam raised his gun. Ryan ducked. The shot rang out, shattering the window into a spiderweb of cracks.

There was no time to think. Ryan charged ahead, shoulder rolling through the broken glass and into the master bedroom. The cloying scent of gardenia assailed his nose as he ran through the dark space, looking for a door to escape. Ryan turned a corner just past the fireplace when a gunshot whistled near his shoulder, striking the drywall in a puff of white dust.

"I need him alive," he heard Elaine yell.

Ryan dashed across a corridor to a set of double doors. He flung them open, his feet echoing across the marble floor in his rush through a formal sitting area. Another set of footsteps were approaching on his right.

Where to go? This house was a maze. Choosing to run straight ahead, Ryan saw a spiral staircase leading down. He reached the top and dared a look over his shoulder. Sam was not far behind him.

Ryan's feet hammered down the stairs, taking them two at a time. When he neared the bottom, he leaped over the railing and landed with a hard thud. Heavy footsteps pounded after him down the stairs. Racing forward, Ryan headed toward a glass atrium filled with large leafy plants, hoping for enough time to hide. Suddenly, there was a pop, followed by a rapid clicking sound. Ryan grunted with pain as tiny barbs bit through his shirt, sending volts of energy coursing through him, forcing his muscles to contract and lose control. He fell to the ground. His only hope was that he had hidden Cassie well enough.

THIRTEEN

Ryan wasn't sure how long he'd been held in the dark room when he heard feet trudge down the stairs. The door at the end of the room swung open, and Ryan's heart dropped into his stomach. Sam entered with Cassie slung over his shoulders, and Elaine followed close behind him.

"Cassie!" Ryan called out, blinking his eyes against the harsh lights that Elaine flicked on. "What did you give her?" He struggled against the shackles holding him to a ladder-back chair, fear ripping through his gut. Sam slumped Cassie against the black steel cabinets in the far corner. *Was she still breathing?*

Elaine eyed him shrewdly. "She's fine for now," she said, walking toward him.

With the lights on, Ryan's eyes darted around the room, trying to evaluate the best escape options. The room was long and rectangular, with no windows. It was wall-to-wall mechanic-grade cabinetry with stainless steel countertops, a built-in sink and backsplash. An exit would only come from one of the two doors that lay on opposite ends of the room, but first, he needed to get out of these bindings.

Elaine opened a lower cupboard, pulled out a suitcase and flopped it noisily on top of the steel counter across from Ryan. "Sam, what's going on outside?"

Obediently, Sam took a remote from a drawer and turned on the wall-mounted TV above Elaine. He stood back for a second and watched the various camera views of the estate's exterior and interior come to life. SWAT members dressed in full tactical gear peppered the driveway with strategically placed rapid response vehicles. The well-seasoned team stood assessing the daunting fortress, its soaring windows now encased by blast-proof security roll shutters.

"I'd say they're about five minutes from breaching the premises," he said, unconcerned. Sam returned to his position across from Cassie and stayed watchful of her movements.

Sliding open a drawer, Elaine casually began pulling out stacks of cash and placing them into the suitcase.

"You really think you're going to get out of

here?" Ryan nodded up at the TV screen. The SWAT team was advancing toward the front of the house. "They're on your doorstep."

Elaine spared the screen a look. "If those men and women out there *really* are with the police, why should they be angry with me? What could I possibly have done? Sheltered an old friend who asked for protection?" She flipped through passports and then picked two, putting them into the suitcase next to the cash. "Cassie escaped from Agent Bell and contacted me for help. After everything she had been through, she didn't trust law enforcement."

"We both know that's not what happened."

"Why would you say that?"

Ryan watched Elaine reach into a cupboard and don a black pair of satin gloves. A knot formed in his belly. She strode over to him, a malicious gleam lighting her eyes. Slowly, she lowered her face to within an inch of his. "All I know is that a friend in desperate need showed up at my door and made a very compelling case as to why she needed my help." Elaine's hand ran over his earlobe. "Then, inexplicably, you showed up." Her finger slid down his neck, dipping below the neckline of his sweatshirt, and caught the chain of his necklace. A smile lit her face. Elaine looped the chain around her finger and pulled it up, letting the cross pendant dangle above his shirt. With a satisfied smirk, she let it fall with a heavy thunk against his chest. "Regrettably, Agent Matherson, you were discovered prowling around my estate where you weren't invited. An action I find very suspicious considering Cassie has just escaped the clutches of a dirty agent. Tell me, Ryan, are you thirsty?"

"No."

Elaine stood up and walked over to the sink. Filling a glass with water, she set it on the counter behind him.

"I'm sorry you feel mistreated. You must understand that the nature of my business creates threats from the most unexpected sources. No agency is immune to temptation, I'm afraid." She ripped the chain from around his neck. "Espionage is likely to come from any source. No one can be trusted." The necklace fell from her fingers into the water. "I just hate eavesdroppers. Don't you?"

"Your lies won't untangle you from what's happening here that easily. We recorded our phone conversation." Now it was his turn to smile smugly. "You know the one where you threatened me for the incriminating evidence against you."

Elaine seemed amused. "One conversation.

You have one questionable conversation taped and you think that is your smoking gun? You called an unregistered burner phone, not my personal one. Even if that wasn't thc case, how hard do you think it would be for me to have your recording erased, or ruled inadmissible in court. You need to remember who you're up against. I'm too smart to lose, Ryan."

Turning her back to him, Elaine walked to the far wall and pulled open both doors of a full-length cabinet. The pantry held an array of weapons: handguns, assault rifles, survival knives, machetes. This woman didn't mess around, Ryan thought.

Elaine took onc of the Glocks from its perch and loaded it like a professional. "I understand she's a Glock kinda gal."

Metal cuffs tore into Ryan's flesh as he leaped forward in his chair. The chair slipped sideways, pulling Ryan with it. His shoulder slammed hard onto the tile floor. "Cassie!" He thrashed against his bonds, not registering the pain. "Cassie! Wake up! Cassie!"

Sam stepped toward him, but Elaine held up her hand, ordering Sam to stop.

"I've got this," she said, crossing the room. Elaine removed Cassie's handcuffs. Crouching, she positioned herself around Cassie, and molded Cassie's pliable hand to the grip of the gun. Elaine braced Cassie's limp arm with her own, forcing her hand to raise the gun with deadly determination. She aimed it at Ryan with trained precision.

"Cassie!" he yelled, but she didn't stir. Her head just lolled to the side. There was nothing more that he could do. Ryan stopped struggling and tenderly watched Cassie, wishing he could tell her that he loved her. He smiled and braced himself for the impact of the bullet.

Suddenly, Elaine twisted like a viper and shot Sam in the stomach.

The force threw Sam back against the wall. Shock flashed across the man's face; his hand fumbled for his gun. Elaine fired off two more shots, hitting Sam square in the chest. Like a rag doll, he slid lifelessly to the floor.

"Why would you do that?" The words fell stunned from Ryan's mouth.

Elaine set the gun down and slumped Cassie back against the cabinet. She walked over to Sam's body, nudged him with the tip of her shoe, then bent down to check the pulse at his neck. "Sam is a dangerous man," Elaine said, wrinkling her nose. "*Was* a dangerous man. Not the sort of person to fall on the sword for their boss. His death makes him a lot more amenable to my way of thinking. Don't you agree?" she said sarcastically.

"What are you talking about?"

"The police will discover that Sam knew all about the code hidden in the painting and that he hired The Wolf to assassinate the congressman. They will be horrified to learn that Sam engineered a nasty computer virus that allowed him a back door into the federal computer databases granting him access to state secrets which, alas, he has been selling."

"You set him up," Ryan said in disgust.

"A smart woman always has a contingency plan." Elaine opened Sam's blazer, careful to avoid the blood, and removed the gun from his holster.

"Your lies don't explain what happened down here."

Elaine walked closer. "I had an awful confrontation with Cassie, where she accused me of terrible things. Upset, I went for a walk along the ocean to clear my head. While I was gone, Nathan found you searching through my office. He called me, and I instructed him to detain you for questioning—understandable considering my line of work. When I got back, I found you and Nathan fighting in the dining room. I saw you hit him with a candlestick, knocking him out. I was terrified, so I stunned you with my Taser. As you were rousing, all these armed men started showing up in armored trucks. I thought the estate was under siege, and Sam was missing along with Cassie. I activated the security shutters and forced you into my panic room at gunpoint to figure things out. When we got down here, we discovered Sam, holding Cassie hostage. I was shocked to discover that he had contracted The Wolf to kill Cassie." She aimed Sam's gun at Ryan. "You were such a smart agent. Somehow your search of my office helped you determine that Sam was responsible for everything. Not me, like you had originally thought—" her lower lip pouted "—but sadly, Sam shot you."

"And Cassie?"

"Well, she's just coming off of a drug-induced stupor, which renders her an unreliable witness. Sadly, Cassie won't be able to discern fiction from reality, and she won't be able to explain the gun in her hand that shot Sam. The only person here with a reliable and reasonable story is me."

Ryan glanced up at the monitor. The SWAT team was laying explosive charges at the front door.

"The police will find me leaning over your body, trying to stop the bleeding." Elaine aimed the gun. "I'll be a hero, Ryan."

He didn't hear the first gunshot. Only felt the pain searing through his chest. A scream ripped from his throat when the second bullet pierced through his side.

"Unfortunately, I won't be able to save you." She put the gun carefully back in Sam's holster. Then, pulling a section of the stainless steel backsplash down, she stashed the gloves and shut the compartment.

Pain overwhelmed his senses, and he choked.

"Know your enemy, Ryan. The feds love a hero. They will devour every last bite of what I feed them. While there may be blood on my hands—" she smiled "—there won't be any trace of gunshot residue to prove I did anything."

Elaine opened a drawer and pulled out a towel.

"I might get a slap on the wrist." She dropped to her knees and leaned over him, pressing the towel just below one of the wounds.

Excruciating pain shot through Ryan, almost making him black out.

"I'll be free to start over. I've got enough power, leverage and friends out there to ensure that."

Ryan's animallike yowl tore through her consciousness. *Ryan!* Cassie's pulse pounded in her ears. Her head lolled to the side. She stared at her arms—arms that didn't feel like they belonged to her body. *Move.*

She raised her eyes and watched Elaine dig her fingers into Ryan's wound. His eyes bulged while he choked back the pain. *Ryan!*

Fury wound like a frenzied wildfire inside her. Her eyes fell on the gun just out of her reach. With every fiber of her being, she begged her fingers to move, but they lay limp and useless. Enraged at her traitorous body, Cassie let her head rest against the cupboards.

Ryan groaned.

I can't just sit here and watch him die. With renewed vigor, Cassie concentrated on her fingers and prayed with a fevered intensity. Memories flashed before her eyes: Ryan's shy smile when he helped her deliver meals to the elderly, his laugh at his own lousy dart throws, the softness in his eyes when he touched her. All these snapshots combined, motivating her efforts to move.

Cassie's arm twitched, sending a rush of victory sweeping through her. She looked over at Ryan and saw an impossible amount of blood pooling around him. Her efforts were not enough. She had to do more if she was going to save him.

Cassie bit her lip, concentrating on her ab muscles, thinking of each one, forcing them to contract. With agonizing effort, Cassie reached for the weapon. She fought against the fog, refusing to give in, and was relieved only when her hand closed around the Glock.

Gasping for breath, she flopped back against the cupboards.

She couldn't quit now. Cassie forced her clumsy hands to rack the weapon. With wobbling arms, she raised the gun. This might be her only opportunity; she had to take it. She fired. Kickback knocked the weapon from her hand, and the bullet went wild, glancing around the room.

Elaine's laugh echoed in her ears while the room teetered before Cassie's eyes.

"Was that meant to hit me?" Elaine scoffed. "I hope that wasn't your best effort to save him."

Nausea rose in Cassie's belly, but she gritted her teeth and reached for the gun. The quick motion threw her off balance, sending her nose smashing into the floor.

"You really are pathetic," Elaine taunted.

Cassie closed her hand around the warm weapon. She pushed herself up onto her hands. "Stop talking," Cassie said, her nose throbbing.

"You can't even stand up, let alone aim. Shoot again, and you're just as likely to hit Ryan as me. You're not that stupid."

Elaine was right. She was not stupid, nor was she going to give up that easily. With the gun in one hand, Cassie gripped the cupboard handle with the other.

"Let go of the gun or I'll make his last moments on this earth excruciating."

Ryan let out a stifled shriek, but Cassie didn't look over.

Instead, she flung a wild arm on top of the cold counter, groaned when she scraped her chest over the sharp metal edge and pulled herself up onto her feet. Cassie glanced up at the TV. Police had broken through the front door and were storming into the estate.

She leaned heavily on the counter, her eyes darting to Ryan's. The dark red pool of blood was quickly spreading into a lake beneath the man she loved. His breathing was coming in short, labored gasps for air. "Back away from him," Cassie said in a voice that sounded stronger than she felt.

"You don't give up, do you?"

"I said back away." Her arm moved a little easier as she steadied it on the counter, coldly aiming the gun.

Elaine's eyes narrowed with the recognition of her predicament. She rose to her feet and stepped backward. "Things would have been so much simpler if you had just died with the congressman." She let out an annoyed sigh.

"Just look at poor Ryan. He wouldn't be in this state if you had followed the plan."

"Stay where you are."

"It's a risky shot, Cassie. Another ricocheting bullet could hit Ryan. Are you willing to risk it?"

A shiver of doubt ran through her. *What if I miss?*

Elaine smirked a mere second before she turned and charged for the weapons cupboard.

"No!" Cassie screamed in a rage-fueled battle cry. She lunged across the room, adrenaline flowing through her legs, making each stride smoother and steadier than the last.

Elaine extended her arm, swiping a knife from its perch in the cabinet just as Cassie sprang.

Cassie's shoulder collided with Elaine's waist, and they fell to the ground in a mix of limbs. The gun clattered across the tile. Their hands and fists grappled as they battled, rolling across the floor. Elaine sliced with the knife, but Cassie caught her wrist, banging it against the cupboard. The knife fell. Reaching, Cassie grasped the weapon and rolled, flipping Elaine onto her back. She pressed the blade to the woman's throat. One slash and this would all be over. No more nightmares, no more looking over her shoulder, no one would blame her.

"Do it," Elaine taunted, the woman's body vibrating beneath her.

One flick of her wrist, and Elaine would get what she deserved.

Ryan gasped for air.

Elaine extended her neck, making her skin taut beneath the blade.

"You don't have the guts!"

Cassie's pulse roared in her ears.

Dearly beloved, avenge not yourselves, but rather give place unto wrath: for it is written, Vengeance is mine; I will repay, saith the Lord. The scripture came to Cassie's mind as visceral as if it had been spoken out loud.

Cassie didn't move. One simple slice.

The memory verse repeated louder, making Cassie grit her teeth. *Vengeance is mine; I will repay, saith the Lord.*

Footsteps thundered down the stairs, but Cassie had already made her decision. Agents burst through the door into the small room yelling, but Cassie felt a sudden wash of peace, despite having a room full of guns trained on her. She lowered her knife to the floor and slid it across the room.

Ryan's eyes drifted open. *Where was he?* Monitors beeped while he scanned the room. Moving his arms, he found wires and tubes taped to them. He looked over and saw Cassie huddled with a fleece blanket; her head flopped to the side of the chair in slumber. She looked beautiful, her auburn hair falling in waves over her shoulder. Cassie's eyes fluttered open like she could feel his gaze upon her skin.

"I didn't mean to wake you," he said, his voice hoarse.

A smile burst across her face as she reached her hand out to him. Tears welled in her eyes.

"I thought I'd lost you," she said, pushing the button on the side of the bed.

"Nurse," she called loudly, making his ears ring.

The glass door slid open with a whoosh. A gray-haired nurse entered and looked at his monitors. "Good to see you awake," she said, adjusting his IV bag. "How are you feeling?"

"Like I went ten rounds with a grizzly bear."

Warmth radiated from her eyes. "That's to be expected." Her hand rubbed his shoulder. "I'll let the doctors know that you're awake."

"Thank you," Ryan said, but waited until the door whispered closed before turning his attention back to Cassie. She was here, and she was alive. Relief flowed through him, and then he saw something flicker behind her eyes. "Will you tell me what happened?" he asked gently.

Her long fingers traced the line of her collarbone, her eyes pulling away from his. "You were shot."

"That's not what I meant."

She exhaled softly and looked over her shoulder into the nursing pod. "I'm not sure that this is a good idea."

"Cassie."

Pulling her eyes back to his, they softened before she took a deep breath. "Okay," she said. "What is the last thing that you remember?"

The question made his ribs ache.

What did he remember? He remembered getting shot. Things got a little hazy after that. "You and Elaine fighting on the floor. What happened?"

Her head tilted subtly, and Cassie's eyes focused on the open window behind him, locking onto the busy parking lot below.

"Let's just say that when the police came in, I had a knife to Elaine's throat."

"That's not a good first impression to make."

"No. No, it wasn't. They had me thrown into cuffs and hauled upstairs for questioning before I could blink." A heavy smile crossed her face. "I was viewed as the principal aggressor, which I discovered the hard way, is not a good label to have. And it didn't help that Elaine was busy spinning her tales in the next room. If it wasn't for Walter, I don't know what would have happened."

"Walter?"

Cassie nodded. "That man sure does know how to take control of a scene. When he came in, agents started taking me more seriously and searched for the gloves."

"You saw Elaine stash them?"

"I did," Cassie said. "And it was something she couldn't explain on the fly. You should have seen it, Ryan. Those gloves were whisked away from Elaine's estate like they were the crown jewels."

"I can imagine."

"Walter said the gloves were taken to this swanky research and support unit at the FBI lab. Apparently, there is some type of chemical fuming they can do on the gloves, and when they combine it with a special light, they can retrieve fingerprints from the silk."

"I thought it was impossible to get prints off of fabrics."

"So did Elaine. It's a costly procedure to have done, but being that she had a congressman assassinated..."

"Money was not an issue."

"Not even a hesitation, from what I'm told. Now the FBI has her fingerprints on a pair of gloves covered in GSR from two different guns. And if that weren't enough, they also found trace amounts of Sam's blood on them." Cassie became quiet.

"What happened to Sam?" Ryan asked. "I'm assuming he didn't make it?"

"No. Neither did Agent Bell. They found his body in the trunk of the car he used to transport me from Eugene to Elaine's estate. Walter said they suspect Sam killed him."

"What about Nathan?"

"He has a mild skull fracture from where you hit him with the candlestick. The doctors say he'll be fine. In fact, from his hospital room, Nathan cut a deal and was going to testify against Elaine."

"Wait," Ryan said. "Did you say *was* going to testify?"

Cassie's eyes met his. "You know Elaine. She thought she was so much smarter than the rest of us." Cassie let out a slow, pent-up breath. "She died trying to escape from prison."

Ryan's eyes rounded.

"She almost pulled it off too. Somehow, Elaine managed to get onto the roof of her cell block. Unfortunately, her makeshift rope broke as she was climbing down from the roof, and she died from the fall."

"That's awful," Ryan said, shocked. He couldn't imagine how emotionally confusing this must be for Cassie. "How are you doing with all of this?"

She nibbled her lower lip. "I'd like to say I'm at peace with it, but I'm not." She dared to look at him and then resumed staring out the window. "Victim Services has reached out with a Christian trauma counselor. I'm going to see her later today."

"That's good." Ryan wished more than anything that he could pull her into his arms. He couldn't stand the distance between them.

She wrinkled her nose. "The counselor and I have a lot of work to do, but with God's help, I know I'll get there."

Needing to be closer to her, Ryan moved to sit up. Pain seared through him like a hot knife, making his eyes roll back in his head.

"Ryan?" Cassie leaped to the edge of his hospital bed.

He gave her a half-hearted smile. "I'm okay." He reached up, tucking her silky hair behind her ear. It felt incredible to be this close to her. "There's something about believing you're about to die that makes things clear." His fingers tipped her chin so that she met his eye. "At the cabin, I never should have left things unsaid between us."

"There was nothing left to say," she said, starting to move off the bed, but he rested his hand on her forearm and she stayed, her head lowering.

“How about I’m not moving to Portland?”

She stared up at him, confused. “But Kate said…”

“Walter and I agreed that I would work for him on a contractual basis. Most of the time, I will be in Bakerton.”

“Oh,” Cassie said, the shock evident on her face. She stood up from the bed and turned her back toward him.

“I love you, Cassie,” he said, unsure what she was thinking, “and I don’t want to waste any more time or let there be any misunderstandings. I love you, and all I want is to be with you. So whether that’s Bakerton or some other place, I…”

“That’s Bakerton,” Cassie said, turning around, tears slipping down her cheeks.

“Bakerton?”

Cassie nodded and came to sit on the edge of his bed. “With Elaine and The Wolf dead, I’m free. I’m free to live my life as I choose—” her hand covered his “—and I choose you. I choose Bakerton.”

“But your family, your art?”

“You’ve just woken up. But it’s been three days, and I’ve had time to think and process. My life is here now, and my family—” Cassie smiled "—I can call and visit them anytime I want to. I love you, Ryan," she said, emotion choking her voice. "I never stopped loving you." She leaned down and gently kissed his lips.

Ryan's heart felt full. His life, one that had come from a place of abandonment, was now brimming with happiness. Everything was different because of God's grace, His healing and His love. God had brought Cassie into his life during a time when he doubted love existed, and, if he were honest, he had done his best to thwart it. For far too long, he had been blind to what God was revealing to him. He, Ryan Matherson, was worthy of love. Inside him, something powerful broke. He could feel its hold wash off of him.

Ryan looked into Cassie's eyes that were shining with joy and knew beyond knowing what he had to say next. He held her soft hands in his. "Wait. I've been unconscious for three days."

"Yes."

"And so that would make today?"

"Christmas."

Ryan smiled. He could think of no other Christmas present that he wanted more. "Cassandra Elenor Roberts, I never want a day to go by without you in my life. I've wasted too much time being a fool, and I don't want to waste one more minute. Will you do me the honor of becoming my wife?"

Her face lit up with joy. "Yes, Ryan. Most definitely, yes," she said, kissing him again.

Not for one second was he going to miss the gift that God had granted him. His eyes were now open, and he was committed to spending the rest of his days loving Cassie without holding back. "Together, forever and always," Ryan said adoringly.

"Forever and always," Cassie said, lacing her fingers with his.

* * * * *

Dear Reader,

Thank you for joining me on Cassie and Ryan's adventure. I had a tremendous amount of fun writing these characters, who at times took unexpected detours from the original plot I had so carefully planned. It's funny how you can be writing dialogue and suddenly realize your character's comments are taking your story in a direction you hadn't envisioned.

Targeted Witness is my debut novel and came about after my husband nudged me to enter a contest for Harlequin's Love Inspired line. He reminded me of the old adage, "till I try, I'll never know." So for all those other aspiring authors out there, and you know who you are, don't give up. Maybe it's time for you to pull your stories out of the drawer and see where the journey takes you. Nudge, nudge.

I hope you have enjoyed reading *Targeted Witness*.

Jacqueline Adam